Sweet Ivy

Janae Willms

Contents

Chapter 1

I 've always been more than just a little "twisted".

Ouma swore up and down that I was worse than the devil, and Oupa cried fat bloody tears whenever he saw me. There were other people who could probably call me much worse- except, dead men tell no tales and you won't ever get the chance to hear their truth.

I casually cracked my neck as I sat in my silent car, in the underground parking lot of the work building that my father owned. Today was another work day, another day where I was forced to be around people I didn't want to be around and deal with their stupid looks. Everyone knew better than to talk to me, Schalk du Toit wasn't exactly the next smiling face of the office, and I've had more than one instance where I've let my twisted side show and ended with bloody footprints all over the office. Pa hated when I dirtied the Persian rug in my office with blood. He said that blood was impossible to remove and he was getting tired of buying Persian rugs every other day.

I ran my fingers over the Bentley sign on my steering wheel and then reached for the door handle, letting myself out. "Fuck. I hate Mondays," I groaned under my breath, pulling out a pack of Marlboro cigarettes as I locked the car and placed a trusted cigarette to my lips. I pulled out a plain silver lighter, bringing it to the cigarette and lighting it as my sneakers pressed on the concrete floors of the underground parking lot.

"Morning, morning, Baas (boss)," one of the security guards, a 36 year old man named Jabu, greeted me as he rubbed his hands together but maintained the distance between us. He was practically on the other side of the garage and I couldn't help but find it comical that he was the one with the gun and all I had was Marlboro cigarettes and a lighter; yet, I'd be the one to cause the most damage- and he knew that.

For a moment as I walked, with my eyes to the floor and my hoodie covering me, I half wondered if I should turn in his direction and get the soles of my new takkies dirty, maybe mess up that Persian rug that pa just bought for his office. I felt a dark smirk spread across my lips at the thought of ending Jabu's life, but I frowned thinking about the new hoodie that I was wearing and how blood took too long to wash out so I continued walking towards the lift, opting to deal with him a little later if I didn't find another victim.

The doors of the lift closed as I pressed the button for the fourth floor, the highest level in the modest building. "Smoking kills. Respect your body enough not to be the cause of your own death," I read the sign inside the lift with my usual raspy and deep baritone voice. I read it every morning and every morning it sounded even more stupid, "I need to find whoever made this stupid ass sign and shove it down their fucking throat," I said deadly, as I continued my smoking. The lift doors opened to reveal an empty floor since it was still early and most of the employees were yet to arrive.

I walked through the floor, making my way to my office on the other end. I saw my name on a golden plank on my office door with the words "Chief Financial Officer" and I opened the door, entering the stale room that I had done very little to design to fit my personality or likes. I didn't like much of anything, I preferred the simple brown table, the laptop in the centre, the neat stack of folders on the left corner and the swivel chair that allowed me a view of downtown Sandton and the influx of trendy restaurants, bars, malls, skyscrapers, fast cars and people.

I walked over to my chair and sat down on it and then let myself face the window like I always do. I got lost in watching the outside world, watching the steady rise of the sun as I finished my cigarette and lit another. I could go days, weeks, months in silence, not bothering to speak to anyone except the voices in my head. I could keep myself going with just myself.

My phone rang- right on time- at exactly 10:25 every morning, and I brought it to my ears, accepting the call after exactly four rings. "Good morning, Schalk," the voice that belonged to my therapist, Pieter came through the speaker and registered in my brain. Pieter's voice was boring, like he worked in customer service and was bored to death of repeating the same sales pitch every day. However, I preferred it to the emotional voices that had belonged to my previous therapists who were mostly women. The 'you can talk to me, Schalk', or 'you can trust me, Schalk' or the 'please! Don't kill me! Help!' the last was my personal favourite.

"Pieter," I spoke, feeling my accent come through even thicker as I spoke to the burly 72 year old therapist who came out of retirement just to deal with the special case that I was. See, Pieter unlike my other therapists knew just how special I was, he knew that there was no changing me. He knew that this was me, and he allowed me to explore myself and my thoughts.

Of course, it helped that he was Oupa's younger brother and we were family.

"How are you feeling today?" he asked me, speaking in the language that I only communicated in, Afrikaans. I hated the language English, I hated the English, I hated those who spoke English, and I hated anything to do with that weak language.

"Good, good," I responded, leaning back in my chair, looking at the slowly burning cigarette between my fingertips as I cleared my throat, "Johannes' girlfriend was throwing some hissy fit today. At breakfast, she started yelling, something about 'what the fuck was wrong with us' and that we were all sick, twisted fucks," I shook my head at the girl's erratic behaviour.

"That's quite unfortunate. Johannes has lost control," Pieter tusked in concern and I nodded my head.

He's gotten weaker.

"I was happy to see him teaching her a lesson just before I came to work," my mind ran back to the image of her screaming and crying, begging me to help her as she ran out of Johannes' room, with a bloodied back from his whipping her. A satisfied smirk comes across my face as I think about the way she was running, her eyes afraid and face scrunched in horrified pain. Soon enough, I was laughing uncontrollably. "You should've seen her face, Pieter," I threw my head back, placing the cigarette back between my lips, "she was so scared..." I said with a deep sigh.

It's been too long. When was the last time we scared someone? I thought, calling out to the voices in my head.

Come on, we don't need to. We're doing so well. We've gone almost 48 hours without making someone scared, a voice spoke up and I wanted to roll my eyes at the only 'good' voice in my head. I gave him the name of Sakkie (Suck-key), it sounds like a pussy name and that's what he is. He's always trying to be good, getting me to stop doing what I love doing. But even if I refer to him as a pussy, he's equally as influential as the others. So his voice gets to me as much as the others do. Thinking of it, I think he's the one who got in the way of me and making myself happy with Jabu this morning,

Shut the fuck up! We need to make someone sacred...how about Jabu? No, he's not good enough, we need more. How about that little lady that ma calls her friend? The one who comes over for wine and gossip? This was the angriest voice that I had, and I called him Ruan. He wanted blood and gore, and the messier it was, the better. He loved to kill with a weapon and the more rusted it was, the better. He wanted screams of horror, and eyes wide in terror- that fed his thirst.

Ma said no more killing her friends, a third voice that had given himself the name of Botha. Botha was the most calculative of them all, he wanted to scare people gradually...slowly, and he loved to drag things out. He loved to take his time, and he encouraged me to savour the moment. We should go for someone unsuspecting...somebody who doesn't know us. Why don't we go for a little drive? Make our way over to that bar across the city and get us a nice girl. A nice Afrikaner girl?

Mmm, yes. With blonde hair, blue eyes, a good head on her shoulders and a knack for having a good time. Yes, Botha, yes... Ruan purred in satisfaction at the idea.

No! Schalk, no. You won't. Sakkie tried to argue the two voices away.

I didn't care for Sakkie today, the other two won. I was craving blood as much as the other. I hummed in agreement to what Pieter was saying as our call hit the 45 minute mark, "I'm concerned about Johannes. I need to speak to him," Pieter said with his usual dead and bored tone as if he wished he could be doing anything else but this. "I'll call you later, Schalk. As per usual." I cut the call and looked at the watch, seeing that it was now lunchtime and I stood from my chair, walking out of the office. I wondered if I should go directly to the lift and make my way to the bar or have some lunch first. I decided to head down to the lunch area and have a bit of something before I go looking for a nice girl.

Any employee who saw me heading in their direction practically raced away, and none met my eyes. It's not like I could meet theirs either way, I kept my eyes low, always opting to not look at any of these people and instead focus on where my feet were leading me. I decided to use the stairs and made my way to the second floor where the lunch area was. Most of the employees would be there but I knew that no one would bother me, they never did because they all heard stories about the boss's son who'd done more than just a few things that had been covered up.

I didn't care to cover it up, I never did. I wanted them to know, I loved the way that it made them fear me. Some thought they were just rumours, others knew better, either way, they stayed the fuck away from me.

I made my way into the lunch area, making my way to the coffee station and making myself a coffee with two sugars before I walked over to one of the tables, one that I always sat at, right at the glass windows so that I could enjoy the view while I sipped my coffee.

Maybe I should get myself a pizza. I thought to myself, thinking about whether I should get food or if the coffee was enough.

Oh yes, the margarita pizza is the best, Botha chimed into my thoughts.

I prefer the pesto pasta, Sakkie said, and I thought about it, suddenly swaying in the direction of the pasta being sold in the mini restaurants that we have in the building.

As I was lost in the thoughts of what to get for lunch, I heard a small voice speak to me. "Hello," I blinked, slipping away from my own mind and slowly turning my head from the window to the young lady who stood in front of me.

She was dressed in a two piece skirt suit, it was a black skirt that reached decently a few inches before her knees with a white oversized shirt that was untucked and a black pair of stockings to appear more professional in a work place setting. She wore a pair of black shiny leather four inch block heels and her hair was in a high bun, with a few tendrils loose on either side of her face. My eyes traced the curves of her hourglass figure, one that looked far more exceptional than any other in the world. She was petite and ladylike in her 5'2 body that felt quite dwarf to my 6'3 build.

My eyes settled on her diamond shaped face, taking in the honey toned skin and an upturned button nose with bottom heavy lips that were painted in light pink lip gloss, not too much but just enough to glisten under the light of the sun. She wasn't wearing much makeup, and her lashes were short but full, perfectly highlighting her warm brown eyes. A nervous smile was spread across her face and I swear, the world fell away at that moment.

I lost all train of thought as I looked at perhaps the most beautiful woman to walk this Earth. "You wouldn't happen to be waiting for someone, would you?" she asked me, her voice was small and angelic- it was delicate, and she sounded like heavenly sin with an angelic face. My dick immediately hardened at how innocent she looked, how bashful she was, the small smile on her face, her voice that seemed to be so soft it was hardly clear to hear in this lunch area. I knew everyone was watching her. She was so stupid, so naïve of the danger that she had placed herself in. "See, I'm..." she stammered nervously, "I'm new here, and I guess I'm just looking for someone to sit with and talk to," she bit her bottom lip and then presented a purple Tupperware, "I've got cookies," she said as if that would sway me.

Suddenly, all three of my voices piped in.

Mine, mine, mine, all mine. Sakkie was the first to speak, his voice suddenly taking a dark turn as he claimed her. He sounded as twisted as us at the moment, possessiveness coming through in waves, and washing over me as his words repeated in my head like a terrible song from a fare.

Fuck, look at her, showing her fucking legs. And that little ass skirt. We have to teach her a lesson, Schalk, she can't dress like that! Teach her a lesson! She's ours, she can't be showing what's ours! Who knows what all these men are thinking! Ruan exclaimed in my head, his anger washing over me along with the possessiveness that I felt.

Mmm, yes...Schalk, she's yours, mine, his...ours. All ours. We already have her. Botha spoke, his voice husky as my eyes raked her figure yet again. She had curves in all the right places, her ass was tight, not too big because I hated those, but hers was just right, it definitely was no Afrikaans girl's plank that they usually had. Hers was shapely and defined, perfect on her perfect body.

I had my own twisted thoughts of taking her, fucking her in front of everyone so they knew that she belonged to me. I wanted to have her choking on my cock with her bamboo shaped eyes looking up at me in fear because she couldn't breathe. The tears that would slide down her face, the feel of her tiny fists pounding against my pelvis as she tried to breathe, but I wouldn't let her. I'd bury myself in her throat, forcing her to take every inch as I gripped the back of her head and thrust into her like the animal that I was. Oh yes, she was mine, mine, mine. Ours...she's mine, Sakkie's, Ruan's and Botha's. She's all of ours.

She belongs to us.

I set my coffee down and weaved my fingers through each other and she smiled, as if that was an 'okay' as she sat down and opened the Tupperware, presenting the cookies, "my granny made these for my first day, so I could offer them to my co-workers and make friends," her shy smile as she peered at me through her lashes, speaking in that darned English that I hate. "Sorry, where are my manners," she placed her head on her palm on the table, her eyes sparkling with a lightness that I couldn't wait to put out, "My name's Ivy, actually it's Zama Ivy Sibiya. But I go by Ivy."

Oh, Ivy. My sweet, sweet Ivy. I'm going to ruin you.

"Schalk du Toit," I found myself croaking out, reaching for the cookies in the Tupperware, "and I go by whatever you want to call me, sweet Ivy." I found myself saying in English.

Chapter 2

I smiled as I made my way to my 2016 Datsun Go that my uncle bought for me when I told him of my successful interview at Thoito which was an engineering consulting agency. To be honest, I hadn't thought that I was going to get the job. I had been an absolute nervous wreck sitting in front of the boss, a Mr Bertus du Toit with a face of stone and a thick Afrikaner accent that I was sure would guarantee that I wasn't going to get the job since I was a young, black woman, who knew very little Afrikaans and he had been forced to change from his Afrikaner tongue to English to accommodate me. The frown on his face made me feel like it was guaranteed that I would never step foot in here again, but I was surprised when I got a call two days later, asking me to come through the following month for my first day at the job.

"Goodbye, Jabu," I waved with a smile at one of the security personnel in the underground parking lot. He smiled at me, looking up from his Mobicel phone with a kind grin on his face as he waved at me and moved his beanie a bit on his head.

"Did you have a good first day, Ivy?" he asked me, standing a few car spaces away from me as I remembered how I had been crying before I entered the building and Jabu had been the one to knock on my window, bursting my little bubble. I rolled the window down, trying to suck in my tears but the moment that the window was halfway down, I practically sobbed, and Jabu had to give me a pep talk on how I had nothing to worry about, how he was proud of me for getting this far and I was a big girl who was going to take over the corporate world.

That was more than enough to make me feel confident for my first day. He walked me to the lift and helped me get to my floor and he had to go back to guarding the cars in the garage, but I had been more than grateful. Which is why I handed him the takeaway of the pesto pasta in his direction, offering it to him. "It was a good first day," I affirmed as he thanked me for the food and then I said my goodbyes, getting into the second hand light blue car that didn't fit in with all the other fancy cars in the parking lot.

I closed and locked the door before I started up the engine and then reached for my phone that immediately began ringing. I laughed, "Kuku, what if I was still working?" I asked her, looking at the clock as it was exactly 16:00. I got off a few minutes earlier because I got a lot of my work done and my supervisor said that I was free to leave, so I did. My grandmother had promised to call me at the exact time that I knocked off. I worked from 8:00 to 16:00 so I knew she had probably been sitting by her phone until the clock struck 4 pm.

"Hush," she laughed lightly, too eager to hear all about my first day. "How was your first day at work?" she asked me as I drove out of the parking lot and made my through the usual traffic, driving a bit further from Sandton to a cheaper part of Johannesburg, if you would even call it that. Jo'burg was expensive, this one just so happened to be R2, 000 (Rand) cheaper than the other apartments which was why I called it cheaper, but really, it was ridiculously expensive.

I droned on and on about my first day, telling her about the meltdown that I had in the car before I made my way inside and about Jabu. My grandma prayed for his kind soul, and cried about how he was a godsend. I laughed and told her about all the people I had met, including the "friend" that I had managed to make with the cookies that she had baked for me.

"Really?" she asked happy that I wasn't alone at work and wasn't ostracized especially since I had noticed that I was only a handful of people of colour in the workplace. So I had worried that I would experience some racism, however that hadn't been the case. Other than the Afrikaans speaking that went about, when I spoke English everyone responded back to me in it so I didn't care to focus on anything else. I was keeping as positive as possible.

"Yeah," I answered her, thinking about Schalk. Schalk was a big man, 6'3 to be exact, and he had a big build. Unlike the other people in the building, he didn't wear a suit but he wore a black hoodie with a pair of black sweatpants and expensive takkies I was sure were unreleased pair of Nike Air Jordan's. I had noticed the black leather simple watch on his wrist and my eyes widened at the signature TAG Heuer Carrera that cost north of R100, 000 on his wrist. He had dirty blond hair that was tousled and reached just before his ears, in a perfect mess that seemed to be organised more than disorganised. His eyes were a dark blue, almost black, except if you paid too close of attention for too long then you'd notice that they were a dark blue. He had an oblong shaped face and a five o clock shadow with an asymmetrical nose with pale ivory toned skin. He was very handsome, but I couldn't help but get chills every time that his eyes met mine.

His eyes never strayed from my own, and it felt like he was analysing every bit of me. It's why I could barely meet his eyes most of the time since I'd be forced to look away, and look at anything other than him. He didn't speak much since I did all of the talking, but I did like him. I mean, it didn't help that he was very handsome but of course, I wouldn't even label it as a crush. He was a fine man, but I was happy that we had gotten quite acquainted with each other by the end of the work day.

Kuku and I talked the entire time that I was stuck in traffic and she told me all about her day; where she just watched a little bit of TV, then sat outside to get some fresh air, then came back inside and slept, then woke up, and finally prepared food for my younger cousins so they could have something to eat when they came back from school.

I missed her. I had been staying with her all my life and had moved out when I had gotten the job, deciding that it was best that I moved from Pretoria to Jo'burg to be closer to work and make my commute a lot easier. I was very much so homesick and missed my two younger cousins who stayed with her as well, and I promised her that I would visit as soon as I could. I pulled into the familiar yard of the lady who had a bit of a 'guesthouse' aka apartment in her backyard in the more suburban parts of Jo'burg. Thankfully, nobody was outside so I wasn't forced to make any kind of conversation. I parked my car under the shade port and made my way out of it, then walked around the home, making my way to the tiny building that I was staying in.

The apartment had one bedroom, one bathroom, a tiny kitchen and an even tinier dining section but I didn't care. It was the first place that I had gotten and if it wasn't for a friend of a friend, I would probably have been commuting between Pretoria and Jo'burg, so I was more than happy about the place. Plus, it was perfect for me. I didn't like big spaces, and it didn't hurt that there was an entire family staying in the same yard as myself. Since I was a single woman, petite and not very strong, it made me feel a lot safer.

The barking of their dog could be heard as I rolled my eyes at it.

That thing hates me.

I got into the house and closed and locked the door behind me before I made my way through it, taking off my clothes as I went. I walked over to my TV and put on HGTV letting it play as background noise as I walked around in my stockings and bra, making my way to the bathroom to shower. I took particularly long showers ever since I started living her. See, showers were a luxury that I had only gotten used to once I moved here which was...2 days ago. So since 2 days ago, I had only showered three times before in my life. Yeah, yeah, don't judge me. I was raised by my grandmother in her two room house and bathed out of a plastic basin most of the time, and the three times I had showered was when I had been visiting my wealthier uncle who stayed in Pretoria North. So now that I had my own shower, I showered until the hot water in the geyser ran out.

I stepped out and when I did, it had become dark outside as the sun had fully set and My Lottery Dream Home was playing. I wrapped myself in a large towel that reached just before my ankles as I made my way over to the TV opting to change it to a movie since it was getting a bit late. I could still hear Tyson barking, except this time his barking was far more intense. He barked a bit louder than usual and I stood there, lowering the volume on the TV as I furrowed my eyebrows, my heart racing a bit as I gripped onto the towel, listening for any noise. Tyson was a loud dog, and I think he got off on barking because he did insistently. However, this felt more urgent. His barks sounded angry and desperate.

Hopefully, Lorna long-time boyfriend would come out to investigate what was causing Tyson to behave like this. But I quickly rushed for my phone, opening the Whatsapp app and texting Lorna.

Hey, Lorna.

Tyson's barking a lot, is everything okay?

Not even a minute later I received a response. We're checking the cameras. Stay put, it's probably something like a snake or something, or a stray cat.

Kwanele will check it out. You good?

I felt myself calm down a bit and I let out a breath. Yeah, I'm okay. Just got a bit nervous.

She responded with a heart emoji and a, Don't worry, baby girl.

I set my phone down but left it on loud so I could hear it if she sent a response, I raised the volume on the TV, just a tiny bit, as I walked around to the kitchen, about to pull out my leftovers from work and warm them up so I could eat them for supper. Koko had been trying to teach me how to cook but I was terrible at cooking, in fact, whenever I even tried to get her to teach me, she'd roll her eyes and just tell me to be glad that I was a beautiful and intelligent woman so that my husband wouldn't focus on the fact that I can't cook, but be distracted by my beauty and brains.

As I was warming up my food, a loud scream suddenly pierced the air. I jumped, recognising the voice to be Lorna's and before I could even think about it, I rushed out of the kitchen and unlocked my door and rushed outside to make sure that she was okay. Lorna hadn't stopped screaming, and I watched as I made eye contact with her two sons, 7 year old Ephraim and 13 year old Godfrey, who were running towards her like I was.

"What-?!" and before I could even continue, I let out a horrified scream at the ghastly sight that had shaken Lorna. Tyson hung from the avocado tree that they had in the backyard.

He had been sliced in the middle of his belly, and his intestines wrapped around his neck. I let out my own horrified scream, my eyes trailing the blood that practically formed a pool under Tyson and five more feet where bloodied boot prints trailed from the avocado tree to the back of my house, and my blood ran cold.

Chapter 3

I sat on the closed toilet lid with the stall door still open since I couldn't act fast enough to give myself some privacy, as I tried to stop my tears. I hadn't stopped shaking since I saw Tyson last night. I would be vomiting if I hadn't already emptied the contents in my stomach. Kwanele, Lorna's boyfriend, had walked around the home checking to make sure that whoever had killed Tyson was gone, and the coast was clear. The boys and Lorna were highly emotional about their dog, and even I couldn't help but be as hysterical and devastated as they were, even though I'm sure the dog hated me. However, what really pulled at my heart strings was seeing how the family of three wrapping their arms around each other as they cried about their pet that had become a part of their little family.

"Hey, are you okay?" I looked up at the voice and found a dark haired lady in a suit standing before me. She wore a two piece skirt suit that was a navy blue with a black corset underneath, and her dark hair loose and in perfect waves.

She wore mascara that had clumped her lashes together and pink lipstick that had been applied over her lips. She had tanned skin and her brown eyes regarded me with concern.

I was still shaking as I sighed, looking at her with teary eyes. "Sorry, it's been a long night." I chose to say, clearing my throat and suddenly unable to stop myself from saying, "someone broke into my yard last night and killed our dog," I chose to explain, knowing that if I went into detail that it wasn't really my yard and was my landlady's with her two sons and her boyfriend of five years, and how the dog hated me but I had somehow gotten used to him in the two days that I was there, and that he was found hung with his own intestines, and there were bloody boot prints that led to the back of my apartment, right by the bathroom window– would be too much of a whirlwind, so that seemed to do.

She gasped, her expression becoming one of horror and sympathy, "oh no!" she rushed to my side and gave me a tight hug, wrapping her arms around my shoulder, "I'm so sorry!" I breathed in her scent of Chanel perfume as she hugged me and then she pulled back. She took a step back and leaned against the stall door, looking down at me as she handed me a tissue and I blew my nose, thanking her.

"Sorry. I didn't think that I'd be in the bathroom crying, on my literal second day at work," I mumbled sheepishly, feeling more than just a 'little' embarrassed. What would she think of me? What if she was one of those office big mouths who'd tell everyone that I was crying like a little girl and then I'd become the laughing stock around these parts? Oh god, I can already imagine them turning me into some kind of pathetic joke or verb– I can imagine it all now, the office jerks saying 'Don't go all Ivy on us now' when someone wants to cry, or those mean girls saying 'OMG I'm feeling so Ivy right now' whenever I'm around or if they're feeling blue on a random Tuesday, or 'I'm this close to pulling an Ivy' which would be innocently stated by some accounting dude who gets frustrated because the numbers aren't matching or whatever accounting talk is, and the whole office would erupt in laughter murmuring 'same, same'. That would honestly be my worst nightmare.

She shrugged, "oh, there's nothing to be worried about. I come by the bathroom and cry sometimes when work gets a bit too much. It happens to the best of us. The other time– when I just started working here right out of Uni– I didn't know how to use the printer. So I had to ask the boss, and when I did, he yelled at me and told me how stupid, and useless, and pathetic I was and 'how dare I interrupt his very important schedule' to ask him something as silly as how to use a printer. I, literally, cried in front of everyone. And not just 'cried', but as in downright sobbed," she let out a giggle and I joined her. "It was so embarrassing. And I couldn't stop crying, but I didn't care. In that moment I really just missed my mum, and I wanted to be home, and this job felt a little too hard and I couldn't take that I didn't know how to use the printer, and my makeup hadn't turned out right– so there was a lot going wrong. Anyways, it still happens and I've been working here for five years, so don't be embarrassed," I couldn't help but smile at her, feeling myself calm down a bit. Even though my hands still trembled from fear.

"My name's Ivy." I introduced and she nodded, crossing her arms under her breast.

"I know, the office is a small place. We all know each other, and everyone's been talking about the new girl," she began before she continued by introducing herself, "my name's Reeva."

I was suddenly shy realising that everyone knew about me, "everyone's talking about me? Is it...is it bad?" I asked her, wondering if they were being mean to me. I know I shouldn't ask, in case I get my feelings hurt but I couldn't help but really want to know what they all thought of me.

She cleared her throat and stepped back, looking around the bathroom to make sure that there was no one here. When she was sure the coast was clear, she closed the distance between us and dropped her voice a few octaves, "okay, listen. You're new and you don't know any better," she leaned in, her brown eyes looking into my own with what was panic and worry, "But we all kind of stay clear of Schalk du Toit. We all saw you sitting with him, and..." she seemed to struggle to speak as my eyebrows raised in surprise at what she was saying, wondering where she was getting at. "Listen, Schalk's got issues. Like, mental issues. And yes, I know, I know, we have to be sensitive to mental issues, trust me, nobody gets it more than I do." She rushed to explain, "But Schalk is worse, like, really bad. Trust me, Ivy, Schalk's done some very serious things. His mental issues are very...deadly."

"What do you mean?" I asked in a whisper, looking at her, mirroring her expression since I was hanging onto every word.

"I mean, you have to do what we all do, and steer clear of him." At that moment the door to the ladies bathroom opened and Reeva stepped back, making sure to put a bit of distance between us and changed the topic to asking me if I was alright and helping me up. I fixed myself up and Reeva left the bathroom, explaining that she had been gone too long and her supervisor was going to give her hell for it.

I made my way to the mirror and looked over my appearance. Today I wore a pair of black pants and a simple sleeveless beige turtleneck with a necklace around my neck and a pretty silver bracelet around my wrist. I walked out of the bathroom and made my way to my little cubicle and sat down, getting to work on my stuff for the day, trying to do as much work as possible to forget about Tyson. Reeva's words echoed in my mind, occupying most of my thoughts as I sat there until the hours passed and it was lunch time.

I hadn't even realised that it was lunch time, and only looked up when I saw an intern call for my attention. He stood there nervously as he looked down at me and I looked up at him, "erm, Mr du Toit wants to see you in his office. The CFO."

"Oh?" I said in surprise but found myself nodding, "okay, where is it?" I asked the intern.

"Fourth floor, the office right at the end. It's labelled, so you won't miss it." I nodded my head.

"Thanks," I said as I rushed to my feet and made my way to the lift, refusing to use the stairs with my heels on. I nervously stood there, bouncing from foot to foot as I thought about why Mr du Toit would want to see me, the CFO? Oh god, are they firing me. Would they tell me they have no space in their budget for me? Oh god, I'll have to move back home to be with my grandma again, and then what? I can't just eat her pension money, not anymore. She already has so much to worry about and I don't want to make it worse.

The fourth storey was fancy, you could tell it's where the big bosses were. From the marble flooring, to the dark tinted glass walls and fancy planks on their doors. It was nice, very nice.

I walked to the end of the hallway and found the door except the name Schalk du Toit was what was on the plank. Oh shit, how did I not piece together that he was one of the big bosses? Du Toit, duh! Oh no, he's about to fire me.

I knocked on the door and heard a 'come in' in response so I entered the room and closed the door behind me. Schalk's office was exactly like him. It had a simple brown desk, a single chair that he was sitting on and nothing else. I looked around the room and then my eyes were drawn to his dark blue ones, feeling the hairs on the back of my neck stand at how he watched me blankly, "you called for me?" I asked him as I closed the door behind me and walked into the room, my hands gathered in front of me nervously.

"I called you here for lunch," he said easily and I stood there, silent, at the freshly prepared plates of food on his table. It looked like it had been prepared by a chef and brought to him, and it was presented on beautiful white and silver plates with sparkling silverware placed beside each dish. I took it all in, before I nodded, a bit nervous but pushing my doubts to the side since he was the only person who gave me a chance yesterday and we had kind of bonded a bit.

"Okay," I looked around, "where do I sit?" I asked since there was only one chair and he was sitting in it.

He looked at me with a ghost of a smirk on his face as he easily leaned back in his chair and then placed his hands on either side of the chair, "on my lap, soet Ivy," he answered sticking his tongue to the side of his mouth as my lips parted in surprise.

"Wh...wha..."

He didn't respond, only watched me with a beckoning gaze and I felt my heart race at the way that his eyes drank me in. Even with the pants that I wore– the straight-leg pants that didn't reveal as much– I felt like I was standing before him in nothing but skimpy lingerie. Goodness, was it hot?

I swallowed the rest of my words as my legs found themselves making their way to him and I stood in front of him, looking at him nervously. He placed his hands on my waist and pulled me to him, placing me with ease into his lap and I took in a sharp breath at feeling his body so close to mine. "I do-don't think," I stammered, trying to put my thoughts together but he wasn't listening instead he was reaching for one of the plates, picking up one with spaghetti and then easily slid the fork through the thin strands of spaghetti and then twirled them around the fork, "th-this is a good idea," I suddenly found the words, swallowing, as he lifted the fork to my lips, some strands of the spaghetti dripping from the fork.

"Open up, my soet Ivy," he croaked out lowly in my ear. His face looked down into mine, his lips only inches from my ear and I shivered. I gripped onto the material of my pants, suddenly trembling. I don't know if it was from fear or the very effects that his dark and deep baritone bass voice had on me that I struggled to think of anything to say.

I looked into his eyes, trying to see the humour and trying to see if he was joking with me. I didn't know what else to do except what he was asking since the fork was inches from my lips. I parted my lips and opened my mouth. He brought the spaghetti to my lips and into my mouth and I wrapped my lips around the fork, taking the food into my mouth as a rebellious strand of spaghetti hung outside of my lips as he pulled the fork out. His eyes had seemingly darkened into the darkest shade of black I have ever seen, "yes...good girl..." he let out in a dark growl as I slurped the spaghetti into my mouth. He watched me hungrily, picking up some more spaghetti with his fork, "open up for me, babygirl."

"Schalk, plea–" I tried to protest for him to stop feeding me, but he just shoved the fork into my mouth and this time, more than one strand of spaghetti hung from my lips.

His eyes greedily drunk me in, taking in the action of my puckered lips as I attempted to eat the spaghetti that was quickly filling up my cheeks. My desperate fists gripped onto the edges of my pants as I sat there, trying to calm my racing heart and my heated face from what was happening. The way that his dark blue– well, now, black eyes– watched with nothing but pure unfiltered lust the way that I slurped on spaghetti, caused me to fidget in his lap, making me brush against what I was praying was his phone in his pocket.

This is what Reeva must have been talking about. Or was the man just a pervert with money and managed to get away with being called mentally unwell? I don't know, but what I do know is, I'm terrified.

He brought more to my lips, attempting to continue feeding me but at this point I was sure that I looked like a chipmunk with how full my cheeks felt and I was struggling to chew on the food. I tried to chew as quickly as I could, but I was a slow eater; always had been. "Sc-Schalk, pl-please," I stammered, feeling my eyes burn with unshed nervous tears, "I'm not-t d-done eat–" I attempted to appeal to him to at least stop feeding me as quickly as he was.

He seemed to be lost in his own mind, watching me with a hunger that made me feel like he didn't need to see me naked in order to be aroused. He looked at me in the way a predator observed its own prey. It was unnerving– terrifying.

I have never felt any smaller than I did at that moment. I felt weak and tiny in his lap as he towered over me. My face only reaching his chest, his big arms on either side of me, his lap as comfortable as a couch, powerful and firm thighs under my body weight as his eyes glazed over, "You're not trying to stop me, are you, my Ivy?" he asked me, his voice coming out dark and twisted; daring me to say that I was attempting to stop him from force feeding me.

I froze, my eyes widening and my heart skipping a beat as a cold chill ran down my spine at the look that he gave me.

I found myself shaking my head, quickly trying to take back what I said as I let go of his wrist that I had been holding onto. He paused for a moment before he brought the fork to my lips and I parted them yet again, letting him continue filling up my mouth. This time I couldn't slurp on the additional spaghetti that hung from between my lips, since I was trying to chew what I had stored in my cheeks.

He set the fork down, and then I felt him place a finger under my chin, making me look up at him. I done so with glossy eyes, trying not to cry from the fear that I was feeling. He didn't seem to be moved as his dark eyes seemed to drink in the sight of me with sauce all over my lips, cheeks and chin, filled cheeks with food, and struggling to eat, as I was practically choking. He leaned down, closing the distance between us as my hand formed a fist, grabbing onto the material of the hoodie that he was wearing as I felt his tongue along my lips.

I would've gasped if I could have, but instead I froze. His warm tongue moved along my lips, capturing the strands of spaghetti I hadn't managed to slurp up, and eating them for himself as he continued on cleaning my cheeks and chin of the sauce that I had all over me. The tears escaped me then, my legs quivering in fear as I let out short breaths from my silent crying as he continued licking my lips, seeming not to stop even as I kept them pursed, "oh, you're so sweet," he growled out, "spaghetti sauce has never tasted better. I particularly like the saltiness from the tears," he pulled back and then looked down at me as I kept my eyes on his. "Look at you, choking, on a little food," he tusked, "my little good girl. You'll always be choking when it comes to me, soet Ivy."

Chapter 4

I knew everything about her; my little Ivy. My poison Ivy.

Her parents Dorothy Modise and Zweli Sibiya were lovers for a couple of years; four years to be exact, and in those four years they had one child. At the time, they were only 18, and after having Zama Ivy, their relationship ended. Zweli, her father, ended up going to study Engineering at the Tshwane University of Technology, but dropped out after failing because he partied too hard and cared more for entertaining girls than his own studies. How fucking pathetic. After dropping out of college, he had a series of piece jobs, trying to maintain the lifestyle of partying, booze and loose women in cheap taverns, until he ended up being a taxi driver. He had no relationship with his daughter– as a matter of fact, for her graduation he had gifted her R50 and a hearty hug outside the gates of her grandmother's house while he reeked of Heineken.

Dorothy Modise was no better. Dorothy studied to become a nurse, and unlike her 'baby daddy' actually succeeded in completing her studies. However, Dorothy didn't have a single motherly bone in her body and opted to give her child to her mother to take care of and raise. Dorothy lived a comfortable life, as if she were a childless woman, and entertained men. However, she was currently in an 8 year long relationship with some useless bum who drove her car like it was his, and kept her cards on him since she was so blinded by love she didn't care that he was taking care of his other 'baby mama' and their two children. Dorothy did send a little money at the end of every month to her mother to help with the expenses of raising her child; on the 27th of every month, she hand delivered R1, 500 and a McDonald's happy meal. The only quality time she spent with my darling Ivy was during Christmas, New Year's and Ivy's birthday which she had forgotten several times over the years.

Then came the only person who really cared for the object of my obsession; her grandmother, Teboho Modise who had raised Ivy, and two of her other cousins who were the children of Teboho's youngest daughter who had taken after her sister Dorothy. Teboho took care of her grandchildren using her pension money, and lived in a beige two room RDP and had a boyfriend she had met at church.

Teboho spoiled her grandchildren and took care of them as well as she could, which was why my darling Ivy couldn't cook since her grandmother insisted on always cooking. It also explained the several neat Tupperware's in her fridge with meals for the week ranging from Monday to Thursday. Friday's and Saturday's were takeout days for my soet Ivy, and Sunday she would have to make her way to Pretoria for lunch and her weekly meals that her grandmother would prepare for her.

Ivy was mostly taken care of by her uncle, Lincoln Modise, who had finished school, went to university and obtained a degree in teaching and went on to teach for 13 years before becoming a principal at an all-boys school in Pretoria North– working his way to a healthy middle class lifestyle with his wife and two children. If it wasn't for Lincoln, Ivy would've never had the opportunity to pursue her tertiary education since it was through him that she had gotten an all-expenses paid bursary.

I know everything about her.

I know that brown is her favourite colour, and I know that she loves oranges but hates peeling them so she always cut them in fours. I know that she believes that if she eats a watermelon seed then a watermelon will grow inside her stomach, and I know that she likes using the phrase 'were you raised in a barn?' whenever someone leaves the door open. I know that she has a love hate relationship with her hair dresser because the lady didn't exactly have a gentle hand when it came to her delicate head– which is something Emily will pay dearly for– and I know that she hates being alone so she always leaves the TV on as background noise.

I know that she had her first kiss by the graffiti wall across the spaza shop just five houses down from her grandmother's home, and I know that she hates walking that very same corner on the weekends since boys would linger there and catcall. I know she calls the Somalian shop owner 'my friend' and I know that she loves buying Eclairs sweets. I know that she failed Economics 110 and studied so hard her hair fell out so she could get a distinction during her second semester for Economics 120, since she hated the way that Lincoln had sadly sighed at the looks of her report after her first semester.

I know that when she laughs really hard, she snorts, and I know that her celebrity crush is Trevor Noah, which explains why the first boy she kissed– back when she was 15– was a coloured boy who almost looked like Trevor. I also know that she retweets more than she tweets, and I know that she uses a toothpick to clean under nails.

I knew everything about her, because she was ours.

"Look at her," I spoke as I stood over her and watched her sleep, "she's perfection..." I trailed off, looking at the dim lighting being produced by the lamp by her bedside. The distant sound of the TV playing a Nollywood movie that had been set on a low volume met my ears as I stood in her apartment in the dead of night. The numbers 02:13 flashed on the alarm that she had beside her lamp as I reached out a hand and caressed her cheek.

I looked over her, taking in her attire. She had kicked her blanket to her feet, and she was wearing a pair of black panties and a white tank top. I bit my lip, feeling my cock harden in my sweats at the sight of her left boob spilling out of her tank top, and her legs wide open as she laid on her back. My eyes trailed over the inches of her face, my fingers moving as they traced her delicate features that had relaxed now that she was asleep.

She sleeps like a rock, I thought with a smile as my thumb stopped at her lips and I immediately thought back to yesterday's lunch date with her. The way that he lips had wrapped around my fingers as I fed her the spaghetti, and how she sucked on the long strands, her lips forming a perfect pout as the spaghetti disappeared inside her mouth.

I reached my other hand into my sweatpants, freeing my cock into the open air. It was already hard, hard as a rock– it was always like that when it came to my sweet Ivy. She made me so hard I felt like I was 14 again and just found out about porn and masturbating. I didn't care though as I began to stroke the head of my member, my thumb brushing over the tip as I sucked in a breath, my eyes not once leaving those delectable lips as I imagined them around my cock. They were plump, warm and full, so I pictured the light gloss that she would have on them as she'd gaze up at me with those wide eyes of hers– struggling to take me in and down her throat

"Ah, fuck," I said with a satisfied groan as I continued to roam her body, letting my thumb and index circle her little brown nipple and I began to pump my cock. I smeared my precum along the length as I tugged on the little warm bud, making it hard, and began to lightly graze the tip of my finger along the piece of flesh.

Suck it! Suck on her little nipple, I want to taste her. Botha snapped, and I knew that she was driving us wild. Who was I to deny Botha the pleasure? I leaned down and wrapped my lips around the little bud, letting my teeth graze it as I flicked my tongue over it and began to suck.

Oh...yes. I can't wait to suck on them all day, every day. Sakkie spoke up, his words coming through in a satisfied moan as I felt my eyes close in content at the feeling of her titty in my mouth. My other hand had stopped moving against my cock so I slowly resumed pumping, taking my time as I imagined the different things that I would do to her.

Ruan came through next forget sucking, I want to grip on them when we fuck her from behind! We can use them as stress balls, grip onto them, slap them, and tug on them, until she cries, until her little nipples bleed. Suck on it harder, Schalk, suck on it until she fucking bleeds! Even if she wakes up, we'll just fuck her, and make her ours.

I heard her let out a little sound, something like a moan and a groan at the same time. It was soft, but it was there and I felt a smile spread across my lips as I detached my lips from her nipple and spat on the nipple instead. "Oh, baby..." I threw my head back, my movements around my member becoming more determined as I felt the way that I was reaching the familiar high when it came to her.

I left her little wet nipple, trailing with my saliva, and made my way to her panties. I slid them down her thighs, revealing her pretty little pussy that had just a bit of hair on it. Ruan, Botha and Sakkie went wild in my head, screaming all sorts of things at the sight of our haven, at the sight of what was ours.

Slap her little cunt! Play with that clit, make her wet for us! Botha snapped, practically growling as he said those words and all I wanted to do was just that; make her wet, slap that little pussy and play with her clit while she cried out and begged me for more.

Oh what a pretty little thing it is... Ruan croaked out, his words coming out soft yet holding admiration for what was ours. I bit my lip, pumping my member at the sight of her pussy lips and I went to spread them, watching the light pink between her pussy lips and the tiny little clit buried in between. I could picture just slithering my cock up and down her clit, slapping it against the little nub. Or even being on my knees with my lips wrapped around it as I sucked on it and she'd be stuck between pulling my face closer and fighting to push me away because the pleasure would be too intense. I don't plan on being gentle, ever.

Her little virgin pussy is ours. We'll be the first to take her, the first to make love to her. Sakkie spoke up and even I rolled my eyes at the end of his sentence.

Fuck making love to her, we're going to fuck her. I don't plan on being gentle, how dare she tease us like this?! Oh especially that first time, she'll be crying, but so tight, she'll be so tight...We'll probably just bust when we squeeze the head in. Botha grunted, his voice thick with lust as I pumped faster now, my movements becoming more frantic at all of these thoughts of taking my little poison ivy and making her mine, and her tight cunt and her nipple that still glistened with my spit.

"Oh, fuck..." I let out a moan, letting the thoughts of the perfect specimen in front of me take me over the edge as I placed my cock on her lips, slapping the head against the soft pillow of her plump lips. "You drive me crazier than usual,"

I pumped, feeling my balls squeeze and then I grabbed a fistful of her sheets, letting out a deep groan, "fuck!" I let out in an angry groan as I felt myself cum, ropes of my semen escaping the mushroom tip. I aimed my cock at her lips, watching the white shots stain her lips, and then I aimed at her nipple, watching the ropes of cum cover my most favourite parts of her. "Oh yes, oh yes," I said with a groan as I parted her pussy lips again and aimed at her clit, slapping my cock on the flesh as the final white rope of semen fell onto the little light brown clit amidst the pink, and then I let out a smile.

I pulled out my phone, "you look like art, my sweet Ivy," I said as I snapped a picture of her clit with my white cum, and her nipple and her lips that were stained the most. I straightened up and put my phone back into my pocket, and then reached for my still hard member and tucked him back into my boxers as I turned away from her and walked around her little apartment.

I chuckled to myself, grabbing a few things and setting them in different places to drive her crazy. I moved the remote from the couch and put it near the microwave, and then moved the folders from work that she had set on the coffee table to the counter top, and moved her milk which had been placed in the top shelf in the fridge to the side shelf.

I walked back to the door and opened it, closing it behind me and then closed the burglar gate, locking it. It was too easy to pick the lock. I had learnt how to pick burglar gates when I was 15 years old from one of the garden boys that worked on Ouma and Oupa's yard, and it had been easy ever since. I slowly peeled the orange that I had found in her apartment, looking to the tree where I had hung the dog, shaking my head as I whistled lowly, walking and peeling the orange, throwing the peels to the floor as I walked out of the yard and to my father's 4x4 Ford Raptor.

Chapter 5

I was terrified, like, straight to the core level of terrified. I was sure that I was losing my mind as I sat in my car, with my lunchbox in my lap since I now dreaded entering the very building I had been so excited to work at. It felt like things were going haywire, and I couldn't explain it to anyone because it felt a bit like paranoia and I wasn't sure that there would be anyone who'd be able to help.

Firstly and most importantly, yesterday's lunch with Schalk had been...unnerving and concerning. He had me sit in his lap as he fed me food, and he licked my lips clean, watching me like he wanted to devour me. Secondly, when I woke up this morning, the little things around my apartment seemed to not be placed in the usual places that I leave them at. I assumed that I may have accidently left my remote and folder in a different place than usual. I chalked it up to fatigue but I know my mannerisms. To add on to that, I had exactly three oranges left before I fell asleep, and when I woke up I had two oranges left? I had an orange for every day of the week, and I ate an orange a day. I was sure of it. To make it even worse, when I was leaving for work, I found orange peelings all the way from my front door to the gate.

Strange things were happening in my apartment and all I could think about was how Lorna was the only one with access to my apartment since she has the only other spare key. I can only pray that it's Lorna and not her boyfriend that may or may not be entering the apartment when I'm not there.

Basically, things were getting weird and I was scared and squeamish about it all. It was just my luck that things were getting so eerie during my first week of living alone. I kept dismissing my concerns, telling myself that I was overreacting.

Maybe I'm the one who ate an extra orange yesterday when I was coming back from work, or I don't know, maybe I've been so exhausted from work and distracted by Schalk that I keep forgetting where I put my things.

I kept praying that I was doing things subconsciously because I worried about what the truth could reveal. If Lorna was the only one with the spare key and there were no signs of forced entry into my home...then it meant that it was either her or Kwanele. I didn't want to think about it, but the chills that ran down my spine were an obvious sign of how thoughts like this were unnerving me even further.

If it wasn't work, then it was home, if it wasn't home, then it was work.

I sighed and leaned over to the radio, playing Lady Zamar's Collide, as I increased the volume a bit to drown out my thoughts. I reached into my lunchbox pulling out my orange that I had already sliced and took one of the four slices into my mouth, creating an 'orange-ey smile'. I looked at myself in the vanity mirror in front of me and laughed, watching the outer corners of my eye wrinkle as I entertained myself with silly faces.

I didn't think that I'd be spending my lunch break hiding in the car because I didn't want Schalk to find me. I finally understood what Reeva meant when she said that Schalk has serious issues. Schalk definitely has more than a few screws I–

The sound of tapping on my window pulled me away from making silly faces in the mirror, and with the orange still stuck on my teeth, I turned my head to see who it was, feeling my blood run cold as I met a pair of dark blue eyes. He tapped on the window, his taps slow and creepy as he gave me a bit of a smirk when we made eye contact before he waved his hand. He gestured with his finger for me to roll the window down.

I spat out the orange and instead of starting up the car and speeding the hell out of there, I rolled the window down, "..." I prepared to speak but nothing came out as I looked over his features. He had his other arm on the roof of the car as he bent down to be at eye level with me.

"You avoiding me, babygirl?" he asked me, his voice croaking out the words and causing a chill to run up my spine as I quickly shook my head.

"N-n-n...no," I stammered, my voice trembling.

His blue eyes ran over my features as if he could see right through my lie, and a smirk appeared on his lips. "How about lunch, my soet Ivy?" he asked, tilting his head. His voice let me know that it wasn't a suggestion, he was telling me.

I hated it when he called me that because it made my blood run cold. There was a possessiveness that dripped from the words every time that he called me 'his sweet Ivy' and it made me feel as anxious as his unyielding stare. He made it sound like I was his– like I belonged to him and only him. To be quite honest, it made me feel like a toy; a doll.

You know when you're a kid with all your other girlfriends and you all clutch onto your favourite doll possessively and claim 'this is mine' and 'this is my doll' and 'dont touch my doll'? It felt a lot like that.

I swallowed nervously, "I-I al-alread-dy at-ate I-lunch," I tried to pathetically cover up, feeling my heart race because I felt so small compared to him. But he didn't even argue with me, he easily reached his arm into the car and opened the lock, reaching for the door handle from inside as if he knew that the door didn't open from outside.

The air suddenly felt thick and I couldn't breathe in enough of it as I watched him open the door. I sat rigid in my seat, wondering where Jabu was or any of the security personnel. Could I scream for help? Would anybody help me? Schalk was the boss after all, so I was sure that help would be limited.

He opened the door and stepped aside before presenting his hand for me to accept. I wanted to plead for him to leave me alone, but I kept silent and just placed my hand in his, letting him help me out of my car as he closed the door behind me. "My ke-keys," I tried to argue, turning back to the car but he pulled me to his side, his body towering over my own as he held me close and I could smell his intoxicating cologne.

"Don't worry about it. Your car's safe here," he answered me as he walked me further into the underground parking lot. He walked me towards the lift that led into the building, also the place where people of more standing in the company parked. Parking here worked according to who you were. The more important you were, the closer to the lift your parking space was.

He led me to a white convertible Bentley Continental GT that already had the top dropped, revealing white leather seats. The car was absolutely breath taking, and I stood in awe for a moment, my eyes widening because I had never seen a Bentley before. I mean, sure, I see videos of it on TikTok and YouTube, but it was nothing like real life. The car looked brand spanking new as it seemed to sparkle under the fluorescent lights of the garage. "Whoa..." I said under my breath, suddenly thinking to my little Datsun Go and realising the stark contrast between Schalk and I, and I wondered what he saw in me when he had so much. I couldn't even dream of owning a Bentley, it was too damn farfetched.

"Come on," he pulled me to the driver's side of the car, not taking me to the passenger side.

I furrowed my brows as I watched him open the door and sit down, while pulling me into his lap, making me sit across it, "what are you doing?" I asked him, question and surprise thick in my voice as he closed the door behind me and his right arm went behind me, while his left was in front of me as he gripped the steering wheel.

He looked down at me, our faces literally inches from each other as I sat in his lap, thinking about how crazy this was. I tried to calm my racing heart, suddenly feeling my eyes go over every feature of his breath taking face. Schalk was no ugly looking beast, he was jaw droppingly handsome, and the kind of handsome you didn't see too often. From his dirty blond hair and blue eyes, his large build and broad shoulders. He smelled of expensive cologne, cigarettes and pure sin. I hated it, hated being so close to him, seeing the way that his lips curved into a smirk, and the way his breath hit against the side of my face.

He scared me, he did– but, man, was he a sight for sore eyes.

Again, I wondered what he saw in me.

"This is illegal. You can't have me on your lap while you're driving."

As I was sitting on his lap, I could feel his body beneath and beside me. More specifically I could feel his semi hard member near my left ass cheek and I decided not to move at all, not wanting to cause any more damage. Who knows what this man was capable of?

The car was already moving as he reversed the car out of the parking space, not answering me as my legs stretched into the passenger seat. I looked at my kitten heels digging into the expensive leather of his seats.

I was sitting uncomfortably in his lap with my hands by my sides because I didn't know where else to put them. "Come on, relax a little, babygirl," he suggested with a smirk, his blue eyes shining into mine as he dropped one hand from the steering wheel and placed it on my lap as the car stood at the entrance of the parking lot, waiting to merge onto the road. "Put your hands around my neck," he instructed, his voice dropping into my ear as I felt his leg move under my body, pressing on the accelerator and moving forward onto the road.

I gasped at the speed that he was driving, but did as he said. I couldn't take my eyes off of his face, as my arms wrapped around his neck and the wind blew around us. I had my hair in a high bun like usual, but a few of my curls had slipped out and now whipped around me, but even with the commotion surrounding us, I didn't– couldn't break my eyes from his. "Pl-please keep your eyes on the road, Mr du Toit," I threatened as I felt him press on the accelerator even further, feeling the roar of the engine as the power in the car kicked in.

A lopsided grin spread across his lips as my eyes suddenly bounced from his lips to his eyes. His eyes peered into mine fully as I was sure he had pressed on the accelerator fully. However, he kept one hand on the steering wheel, the other on my thigh, slowly riding up my skirt, with the heat of his palm seeping through the material of the sheer stocking that I was wearing, "or what, Mrs du Toit?" he asked me, a dark and mischievous glint in his eye.

My heart was racing uncontrollably against my chest, pounding away as if it wanted to take me out before Schalk did. I was sure that I wasn't obscuring his view since he was so much taller than me, but I was in his lap; he couldn't reach the steering wheel properly and the gear was between my legs, making it easier for his hand to ride up my thigh since my legs were open to accommodate the gear. He was speeding, and his eyes weren't even on the road, they were fully on my own. He wasn't paying attention to anything else besides me, "we c-could die," I stammered, unable to conceal the thick fear and panic in my voice since it hadn't missed me that he had referred to me with his last name.

"Then a glorious death it'll be," he replied, his eyes getting darker with each moment as neither of us pulled away from the other. His eyes were pooled with mischievous lust while mine were drowning with fear and panic. I took in a harsh breath as I felt his fingers now brush against my panties that were a weak barrier between my most delicate area and his large hands.

I bit my bottom lip, shivering under his touch as I felt him brush his fingers against my nether lips. My hold around his neck tightened, my fingers gripping onto a few strands of hair at the nape of his neck as I tried to close my legs but it was to no avail because he pinched the inside of my thighs, "I d...don't think this is appropriate...Mr du Toit..." I let out in a whisper that whizzed by with the wind blowing around us. I wasn't sure if he heard me, but I knew that even if he did, he wouldn't care. "You could kill me." I said, referring to how he was continuing to speed with his eyes on mine and not the road.

"Only if you'll let me," he drawled out as I felt him close the distance between us, his thumb already rubbing against my nether lips with purpose. He brushed his lips against my own, delicately, as if promising me nothing but the death that I was anticipating from his very dangerous stunt. "You're mine, Ivy," he breathed against my lips. Then closed the remaining distance, locking his lips with mine in a filthy kiss with his thumb working against my stocking and my panties, easily affecting me through my underwear.

I didn't kiss back. I sat there, stunned, shifting in his lap at the way that his thumb continued to rub against my panties. He bit my bottom lip hard, and then pinched my clit between his fingers. I gasped, trying to pull my face away from his but he still had my bottom lip stuck between his teeth. "pl..." I tried to speak but the words weren't making sense as I felt tears sting my eyes because he continued to bite me. I gripped his hair, trying to get him to release my bottom lip, but he only bit harder and I let out panicked grunts as I started to cry. The more I tried to pull away, the harder he bit, to the point where it felt like he was trying to rip my bottom lip out with his teeth.

I didn't know how to make it better but in the haze of my panic, tears and muffled screams, I rushed to close the distance between us and locked my lips around his, eager to kiss him back. When I did, he released my bottom lip from between his teeth and began to suck on it as I whimpered in pain at the obvious wound he had left, nonetheless, not once daring to break away from his kiss, letting him do as he pleased with me. The tears continued to flow as his finger working against my clit and he kissed me like I was his last chance to live. He kissed me like I was his prey, a victim to his pleasure and prowl. I didn't even realise that he had stopped the car completely, other cars surrounding us as they overtook us, and we had caused quite a stir as we stopped traffic in the dead centre of Sandton on a random Friday lunch day.

Chapter 6

I took in a deep breath, inhaling the Elizabeth Arden perfume that I had applied that now filled the space in the car. The voices of the hosts of 947 played in the background as I sat in the car, my hands on the steering wheel as I tried to calm my racing mind. It seemed like my life was moving at 200km/h and I could barely keep up. Was this what being young was all about? One moment you're happy you've got your own place, the next you're being pursued by your psychotic boss and kissing him in his Bentley and the next it's the weekend and you hang out with a colleagues over drinks?

Well, shit, it's a lot.

I was still shaken up about what happened yesterday. I wasn't sure what to do, I mean, it was my third day at work, and I already had an issue with the boss. I felt stuck, to be honest. I needed this job more than anything in the world. This job was my big break, and now it felt like hell, and it was only the beginning. I didn't know who to turn to, because

I knew that if I told my grandmother about what was happening with Schalk, she'd demand me to come home, and while I wanted to do nothing more than go home, I knew that it wasn't an option. Kuku had raised me and taken care of me since I was a baby that it was time that I had to return the favour and take care of her. I know how proud she is of me and this job, and I don't want to disappoint her. I don't want to return home empty handed. I know if I told Malome (Uncle) Lincoln, then he'd tell me to report it to HR, but I'm a woman, and I know that Schalk being the CFO and his name owning the company that I worked at, would only make the assault complains disappear, and there's a huge chance that things could only get worse for me. It's obvious that people know what he's capable of, which makes it even harder to envision any more days in that wretched building.

"Modimo," (God) I hurriedly fanned my face as I felt the tears prickle my eyes as I thought about what my life had come to. "Don't cry, don't cry, Zama." I hurriedly rushed out in a sad and strained voice as I cleared my throat, rolling my eyes upwards to stop any more tears. I took in a few breaths, choosing to push my concerns aside and then sat upright again.

I switched off the radio and reached for my phone which was a Huawei P40 Lite and called Reeva. The phone rang a few times before she finally picked up, "hello, darling!" she exclaimed, her voice high and happy and nothing at all the way we usually converse at the office.

I laughed, "hey, Reeva. I'm outside this cute little restaurant called Sippy, could you come get me?" I asked her and I heard a couple of voices in the background before she said that she was on the way.

I looked at myself in the vanity mirror one more time. Reeva had invited me some time in the week to hang out with her and make a couple of friends outside of the workplace, since I had told her that I had just moved to Jo'burg and was all alone, and she said that she couldn't let that happen. So here I was, making sure that the false lashes that I had applied weren't lifting at the corners. I just wanted the lashes to make my eyes look fuller. I preferred not to apply liquid eyeliner, I don't know why, it was just a preference, but I loved the look of lashes on my short eyelashes. I had on a soft pink eye shadow that shimmered, and I had my makeup done to make sure that I impressed them since I was always worried about how I was perceived. And completed the look with a nude lip.

My hair was out of the bun that I usually keep it in and the curls now framed my head. My hair reached just at the nape of my neck, and my hair was dark and perfectly curly, however, it was hell to maintain. I looked down at what I was wearing, which was a short denim skirt that reached mid-thigh with a pair of black leather high heel boots with a floral sweetheart neckline corset that tied in the front.

I stepped out of the car and placed my phone and car keys into the black tiny handbag that I had, throwing it over my shoulder as I suddenly spotted Reeva walking towards me with a grin on her face and a drink in her other hand. "Hey!" she greeted with a happy hug and I returned it as I stepped back, looking her over.

She had ditched the office wear and was wearing a tight leather pants and a pair of platform Valentino heels that I had saved on my own Pinterest board as my dream shoes to buy once I save enough money from my job. She wore a black bralette crop top which allowed her to show off the tattoos on her chest and arms that I didn't know she had. Her black hair was bone straight and held away from her face by the pair of shades she had placed on the top of her head. "You look amazing!" she complimented me as she stepped back and let her eyes look me up and down and I blushed.

"Thank you! But have you seen you?" I replied with the same energy as she slid her arm through mine and led me the way that she had come as we laughed together. "So, how many people are here exactly?" I asked her, getting nervous about meeting new people.

The streets were abuzz as music played from the various chic restaurants and bars that lined the street. It was an amazing atmosphere as I passed all sorts of people, some Goths, some eccentric beyond words, some in suits and dresses meant for the office, and some just plain boring. "There's about seven of us," she explained as she led me into another bar that had the name BARAHOLIC and led me into the place that was buzzing with conversation, laughter and good music.

TOCA by Mi Casa was playing, some people were dancing, others eating, others drinking. Reeva walked me over to a table on the large balcony of the bar, and to a table that had six other people seated, who looked at us when we entered. "Guys, this is my friend, Ivy," she gestured towards me as the other people around the table looked at me, some with smiles, some with curious stares but nothing bad at all, "Ivy, this is the most important person here–"

"Wow!" somebody said, laughing.

"Really?" another said, joining in with the teasing.

"Ouch!"

Reeva ignored them with a grin on her face, "this is my boyfriend, Ricky. His name is actually Richard but he prefers Ricky," she explained gesturing towards a man with tattoos on his biceps, who smiled at me and stood from his seat, giving me a side hug that I returned. He had black hair that was cut into a Mohawk and spider bites. He was wearing a white shirt and a pair of black leather pants and a pair of black CAT boots. He was taller than me, but majority of people are, but he was about 6 feet tall and had brown eyes and a slightly crooked nose. He was drinking from a Savannah beer bottle and seemed to have been enjoying a hearty burger before he stood to greet me.

"Lovely to meet you," he said to me as he sat back down and I was going to respond but Reeva was pulling my attention back to her, introducing the rest of the table.

There was Susan who was a teacher and had a butterfly tattoo on her lower back that she couldn't wait to show me. Susan was a blonde haired, brown eyed girl who was sitting on the arm of her boyfriend, by the name of Steven who– fun fact– worked for the biggest national bank in the country, and in Reeva's words 'maybe you could ask him for a loan some time, and he might, just might, make it happen with the right interest rate' and zipped her lips dramatically as if revealing a secret that I needed to keep on the down low.

Then there was another lady by the name of Precious who was a bald haired black woman with the most dramatic pair of lashes I have ever seen, but she pulled them off like an icon. She had on the coolest pair of hoop earrings that were as outrageous as her lashes, and she wore a tiny black dress that fit her voluptuous body in a way that had to have been sinful. Precious was a marketing associate and apparently worked in the building next to ours.

Then there was Daniel who was Korean, had blue hair that was combed back neatly, beautiful black eyes and baby smooth skin. Daniel was an actuary and worked for private individuals– talk about having a different kind of wealth.

And lastly I was introduced to Benjamin who worked in the same building as us. Benjamin, or as everyone called him, Benny, was an almost 6 foot tall dude with a warm beige skin tone, light brown eyes and a charming smile. He had curly hair that was just like mine, and when they introduced him, everyone immediately began teasing us about our hair because it was the exact same length and the same curly hair as the other, so we were dubbed the husband and wife.

I sat beside him and ordered myself something to eat since everyone else had already ordered, "would you like a drink?" Benny asked me and I smiled, nodding my head and nervously tucking a curly strand behind my ear because Benny was handsome, charming and kind, and I was always shy around guys.

"Oh, yeah, I would. Maybe some Brutal Fruit," and he nod-ded, repeating it to the waiter who walked off and returned moments later with my drink and a glass.

Minutes later, Benny and I had really hit it off. We were joking around and talking about everything. Not just Benny and I, but everyone around the table was entertaining, and they were great, and funny, and super cool, so I didn't regret coming out.

"Ay, ay, ay!" Benny encouraged me as the buzz from my alcohol was suddenly making me dance in my chair to every song that came on, and right now As'Buyeli by Heavy K was playing.

I was an introvert but once I had a little bit of alcohol in my system I became just a 'little bit' extroverted. The dancing had started when I told Benny that I couldn't dance. He didn't believe me, and accused me of being a prude when I watched Precious and everyone around the table smoothly dance in their seats at the various songs that played. "You said you wouldn't laugh!" I accused Benny as I burst out laughing as well, sticking my tongue out and bouncing my shoulders because I thought it would make me dance better.

Benny had tears coming out of his eyes from laughing so hard, "I'm–I'm–!" he couldn't even get his words out as he threw his head back, bellowing so hard that he fell off his chair. "I'm not!" he pathetically stammered in between his laughs but I also couldn't help it as I laughed just as hard, dabbing at my eyes with the napkin that I had. "It's– It's, just, your face! When you stuck out your tongue, I fucking lost it," he explained as he climbed back into his chair and we attempted to calm down. "I'm sorry, I'm sorry," he apologized, a grin still on his face as he downed the rest of his Heineken. "I don't think I've laughed this hard before," he told me as he nudged me with his shoulder and I couldn't help the grin on my face.

I rolled my eyes, "at my expense," I fanned my face, my cheeks sore from laughing. "I told you I couldn't dance. The dancing gene in black people skipped me," I explained to him, causing him to chuckle.

"It's okay that makes the both of us. The dancing gene got washed out by my mum's DNA, we both can't dance," he placed his elbows on the table, our chairs terribly close to each other as we spoke.

I used the excuse of the music having gotten too loud as the reason we were now leaning in whenever we talked to each other, almost in our own bubble. It wasn't anything inappropriate, but we had gotten cosy in the last two hours that we've been here. "I had a good time with you, Ivy," he said to me, our faces close to each other as his light brown eyes looked into mine. The charming smile was back on his face, and I felt shy under his gaze and averted my eyes, causing him to chuckle.

He placed his finger under my chin, making me look back at him as I stuck my tongue to my inner cheek, "don't be looking away from me," he rasped in his voice and I swear I turned several shades of red because of his words as I struggled to not fold under his gaze.

This man... I thought blissfully as I tried to contain the bashful smile on my face.

"Stop it," I complained, bringing my hand to cover my face so that he couldn't see me and he laughed, dropping his hand from my chin.

"Okay, okay, I will. I'm afraid if I continue, you won't have any more feeling in your face," I playfully slapped his shoulder as we both laughed. "But, I hope it's not forward of me to ask for your number, Ivy. I had a really good time with you today, and I'd like us to get to know each other," he said to me, all the laughter dropping from his voice as he spoke seriously to me as if he wanted to make sure that I didn't misinterpret anything that he said. "One on one, just the two of us. It doesn't have to be a date. I think we'd have a lot of fun together, a lot of fun getting to know each other."

I smiled, needing no further persuasion as we shared a knowing smile between the two of us, "Okay, Benny."

Chapter 7

I pulled my car into the shade port, noticing the immediate absence of Lorna's BMW X1. Lorna had informed me, just as we were all heading out around the same time, that she was going to take the kids to the zoo, before wishing me a good day and we all left in our own respective directions. I let out a long sigh, sitting in the car in silence for a moment as I was coming down from the high of being around people who distracted me from what was going on in my life at the moment. I felt my index finger lightly trace my bottom lip, flinching in pain at the memory and wound that Schalk had left behind with his teeth.

I sighed, shaking my head as I grabbed my bag and gripped my phone, going to dial Reeva and tell her that I made it home safe. Distractedly, I dialled her number at the same time as I was removing the keys from the ignition and closing all of my windows, stumbling to shove all the mints that we had gotten from the bar into my bag. The phone rang four times before she finally answered, "Hello?"

I furrowed my brows as my thumb hovered over the key, halfway to pressing the lock button, "Benny?" I immediately recognised the voice to be his. "What are you doing with Reeva's phone?" I asked him, straightening up.

He chuckled, "this isn't Reeva's phone, darling."

"Oh shucks," I gasped, bringing my phone to my face to see whose number I had accidentally dialled, and lo and behold, I had dialled Benny's number. "I'm so sorry," I immediately apologised as I began to make my way towards my apartment, "I thought I was calling Reeva."

"Sure...we can run with that," he teased, as if I was lying.

I flushed, laughing at his comment, "stop, I swear it was a mistake."

"Mhm, or maybe you just missed me so much and didn't want to seem any way and thought to try the 'oh no, I called the wrong number approach'," he continued to tease while I felt my face turning hot as I laughed, shaking my head.

"I swear it was a mistake! I thought I was calling Reeva because she made me promise that I'd call her when I got home," he laughed with me.

"Okay, let me stop teasing you. You must be as red as a tomato at the moment," he said knowingly and I giggled as I dug through my purse searching for my house keys as I stood outside the door. "So, you home safe?" I hummed in agreement as I finally found my keys with all the other one thousand key rings that I had adorned it with. They jingled uncontrollably as I pulled them out and began to unlock the burglar gate first.

"Yes, I did. I'm unlocking the door at the moment." I was still feeling a bit buzzed from the alcohol but it wasn't serious. "Thanks for today, Benny. I had a good time."

"You have less than one minute remaining..." the female automated voice chimed in suddenly.

"You were great company, Ivy–" he began but I cut him off as the door swung open.

"Oh my God, I don't have much airtime left, Benny. I'll s–" I rushed out to explain to him but I suddenly let out a surprised scream as I entered my apartment and sitting on my sofa, sprawled out with his legs wide open and his arms stretched along the length of the sofa was Schalk du Toit. The TV was on and the movie John Wick was playing, on my coffee table right beside the folder of work that I decided to bring home to complete over the weekend was a bottle of half empty Corona.

Schalk sat like he was in his own place, as if it were natural for him to be sitting on my sofa, faced in the direction of the door. He watched me with those unnerving eyes of his, his stare unyielding as it took me in from head to toe. His eyes graced over every bit of skin that I had showing, and I could see the darkness in those eyes spread like the slow slithering of a lazy snake. Bit by bit, his dark blue eyes almost became a pitch black, and I was horrified.

"Wha-what the hell are you doing in my house?!" I ex-claimed in a mixture of shock and fear as he sat there, silent and watching me. My chest felt heavy, my throat tightened and my hands trembled because I knew that this was bad. "G..." I took a moment to breathe and calm myself, forcing myself to be strong, "get the fuck out of my house." I let out venomously, surprising myself with how powerful that had sounded.

He didn't respond, not for a long time, and with each passing moment I felt my bravery leave me bit by bit. Those eyes of his saw right through me. I wanted to turn around and sprint out of there but it's like his gaze compelled the ground beneath my feet to turn into quicksand and I could do nothing but sink. Sink under his scrutiny. "What...what the hell is wrong with you?" I suddenly continued, my voice trembling, "What are you doing in my house? How did you even get in here? Who let you in here? What do you want from me, Schalk?! Isn't it enough that you harass me at work? Ge...get the fuck out of my house, do you hear me?" my fear had changed into weak anger, "I'm calling the police."

My hands trembled uncontrollably as I struggled to see the screen clearly. It felt like I had suddenly gone blind, and my phone in my hands felt like it had been slicked with oil as I struggled to get a good grip on it. My heart was racing a million miles a minute as I tried to think of what the police number was...is it 911? Shit, no, that's the American one. Oh my God, what's 10111's number? 711? I know there's some 1's in there. 081? God, what's their number again?!

"Ivy," he finally said, his voice was thick with malice that I was sure would send me to my grave. As my fingers hovered over the keyboard, they stilled, and I felt my breath hitch at the way that he said my name. The hairs on the back of my neck stood as I kept my eyes on the screen, refusing to look at him. "I'm only going to tell you this once," he paused for just the briefest of moments as I felt my knees buckle under me. "Come to the coffee table and sit on your knees on the floor."

There was no 'please' and no 'thank you'. Just instruction. I began to cry, feeling the hot liquid running down my cheeks, "Schalk, please..." I began to plead, suddenly feeling like even though the door was wide open, there was no actual freedom. The man had been terrorising me since the very first day that we met. I regret ever approaching him with those cookies. I mean, was such an innocent act so worthy of the repercussions that followed? The man was obsessed with me, I was sure of it. "Please...I'm...I don't know what it is that you want from me." I trembled as I looked up to meet his eyes but they were unmoved by my emotional and distraught self. I let out a terrified sob as the room was engulfed in silence, John Wick playing in the background as I wanted to whirl around and run but something told me that if I dared to do that, I would live to regret the day.

My legs moved after what felt like hours of silence, but I was sure was minutes of it. They wobbled as I made my way to the tiny coffee table in the centre of the sofas and the two bean bag chairs. Schalk watched me as I walked towards it, my body shaking so tremendously, it felt like I was going to send myself into cardiac arrest at any moment. I wanted to be as far away from him as possible, so I sat at the other end of the round coffee table, directly across from Schalk as he stared me directly in the eye, his face hard as stone.

I let my body lower, slowly, onto my knees before I sat in silence.

He removed his arms from the back of the sofa and then brought his elbows to his knees, placing them there as he then rubbed his hands together as if cleaning them of imaginary dirt. "Who were you on the phone with?" he asked me, his body leaned forward, his eyes as dark as the abyss, as they looked into my own trembling ones.

My eyes widened in fear, as if I had betrayed Schalk. I don't know why I felt like that. I hadn't done anything wrong. But I knew that me saying that I was on the phone with another guy was going to make him angrier. I swallowed, opting not to respond to him. My widened, fearful eyes peered into his unable to do anything else but stare.

I watched his jaw tick, "babygirl," he croaked, closing his eyes as if he was composing himself, "you have no idea how nice I've been to you. You don't know half the shit that I want to do to you, but today..." I watched as he reached for the bottle of Corona, "you're going to fucking know who Schalk du Toit is, and who the fuck you are to me." he slammed the bottle on the corner of the table, shattering it into shards and I let out a scream.

I jumped, wanting to run out of my apartment but he was quick; so much quicker than me that before I could even jump up, he was standing in front of me, halting any movements of mine as I stood in shock, my eyes wide open. I began to sob and scream. "Schalk, don't hurt me! Please!" I begged him, placing both of my hands up in the direction of his chest as I peered into his eyes, hoping that I could appeal to his humanity but there was nothing there.

He placed a bloody finger to my lips, a shard of glass that he held in his hand brushing against my chin as he did so, "shh," he hushed me delicately, his voice sounding like a melody. "Back on your knees, babygirl, and this time, put a hand on the table." He instructed.

I couldn't stop my sobs as I stood before him, feeling the pain of my neck craning to look up at him as I realised that I couldn't fight him. My stomach sunk and my heart skipped a beat as I realised how powerless I was at the moment. I was at his mercy, and there was nobody here to help me.

The level of fear that struck me then...I don't think there are words to describe it.

I nodded my head, still sobbing, "Please...please don't hurt me." I begged him as I felt my body lower to the ground, back on my knees. I brought my right hand, to the table and then set it down on the cheap wood. My eyes hadn't broken away from his, it felt like my neck was going to snap backwards as I continued to beg him to let me go and not hurt me. I watched as he lowered his body also, resting on one knee, in some kind of power pose, and then in what happened in a blink of an eye, but felt like took two lifetimes to actually occur; Schalk stabbed the shard of Corona glass straight through the middle of palm– so hard, that the glass stuck to the table and my hand was trapped.

I let out a screech so piercing and treacherous, I was sure that the entire suburb had heard me. Crimson blood oozed out of my hand as I looked at the sharp, yet large shard of glass in the centre of my palm, screaming over and over as I felt searing pain overtake every bit of my body.

I didn't see it, but Schalk threw his head back, a smile on his face as I screeched in horror and pain, "ah...my sweet Ivy's voice is just like her...sweet." He had sang with a smile on his face as he let my screams wash over him like the Luke warm water of a shower after a long day.

I felt him place a finger under my chin as he turned my face away from the scene of my bloodied and wounded hand. Tears flowed from my eyes freely, my mouth wide open in silent screams as I looked at him with nothing short of terror, "look at that," he looked at my hand on the coffee table and then back at me, "I've made you bleed." He let out in a fake sigh.

"Are you ready to answer my questions now?" he asked me, but I couldn't even comprehend half of the words that he was saying. My mind was entirely focused on the pain that I was going through that I didn't care, not even a little bit, about what he was saying to me. I guess he saw the haze in my eyes, "I guess not, but there's no need. I already know everything, that little Benjamin you were talking to, I'm going to fucking kill him. What? You don't think I didn't know where you went today, who you were with, what you were doing?" he tusked, wiping away my continuously flowing tears, "I know everything. You know you're mine, Ivy, why do this to yourself?"

He stood up and walked back to the shards of glass on the floor from the Corona beer and grabbed another piece, "No! No! Please! Schalk, I-I'm sorry! Please! No!" I screeched, watching as he looked at one of the pieces in thought and then looked back at me. "No more glass, please!" I sobbed, begging for my life.

"No more glass?" he repeated, in thought and then nodded his head, dropping the shard and then standing upright, "no more glass." I watched as he reached into the pocket of his black jeans and then pulled out a pretty brown piece of wood that I wondered what it could be, until he pressed a button and several sharp blades appeared.

I began to sob harder, begging for him to not hurt me. I kept screaming how sorry I was, and my eyes swelled up with so many tears that my lids felt swollen shut, "shh," he hushed me again, leaning down and kissing me on the lips in a gentle peck. His eyes stopped, looking at my lips where the makeup was now ruined because of my tears. He could see the wound clearly now and I watched as he smiled at it and then looked back into my ears, my pleas now silent.

"Now, I'm going to pick a blade," he told me, and I sobbed, shaking my head, "yes, yes. I'm going to pick a good blade, one that's all jagged and rough, not like this one," he gestured to one that was smooth and would probably be a clean cut, "because I like to make a mess, and I need to make sure this hurts."

"N-no, no, plea…" I begged him, my sobs desperate and broken as I began to hyperventilate while I watched as he picked the scariest looking blade from all of them.

"You betrayed me, my Ivy." He argued, almost with a sad pout on his lips as I shook my head so hard I was sure I'd get whiplash.

"No, no, I didn't. Schalk, I swear, I didn't betray you," I sobbed, begging him. "Please, believe me. I would never betray you, Schalk," I swore, desperation and fear oozing off of my words like hot honey.

"I'm going to do one of two things, babygirl, and since I picked the blade, I'll let you decide which body part of yours I'm going to slice off–"

"No! Schalk please!" I sobbed, gripping his wrist with my left hand as I prayed that he would just let my pleas get to him, "please! Schalk, I'm sorry!"

"Do I slice off your tongue for even daring to speak to another man," he pressed the blade to my lips, taping it twice, "or do I slice off your right ear for daring to call him?"

I shouted, "It was a mistake! I thought that I was calling Reeva! You have to believe me Schalk, please!"

"Tongue, or ear, last chance, babygirl, because if I do it, I'm doing both. So, tongue, or ear?"

I continued sobbing, trying to get away from him now but my hand was stuck on the coffee table and there was no distance between the two of us as he watched me. The blood from my hand had now spilled onto the floor, dripping and dirtying my knees with the crimson warm liquid as I prayed that God could get me out of this. Maybe Lorna or Kwanele would appear at any moment, or the neighbours called the cops and they would arrive and take this man to prison, or better yet, hell. But none of that happened, nobody came to save me.

I knew he wasn't lying which made my cries more horrific, even to my own ears; I couldn't recognise them. "E...ea-ear,"

I stammered, having come to that decision and he nodded his head, reaching his arms out towards me but I attempted to scurry away. However, it was no use, because he got to me and turned my head the other way to get to my right ear, which was the ear that I had placed my phone at.

I began to kick and scream but that didn't deter him, "Schalk, please! Please! Please!" I screeched, feeling the blade on the top tip of my ear.

"Do me a favour, babygirl, make your screams sweet for daddy," he purred before he began to cut at my ear as if he were slicing a stubborn piece of meat. I let out screams so horrid that I was sure would echo the streets of this suburban town for decades.

Chapter 8

"**S**leep my child, sleep softly, under the roses tonight.

First your arms around my neck, and then warmly covered in bed," I awoke to gentle singing, lulling me away from sleep as my heavy eyelids parted in lazy effort.

"Early tomorrow, God willing my child to wake. Early tomorrow, God willing my child to wake.

Sleep my child, sleep softly, with Angels at watch. They show you in a dream, Baby Jesus's tree. The deep silky voice continued as I let out a pained grunt at the raging headache that immediately greeted me.

I felt the soft kiss of a pair of lips on my cheek before the voice continued singing, "Sleep softly, as they show you Paradise. Sleep softly, as they show you paradise."

I closed my eyes at the feel of his lips on my skin, and the way that dominant and strong voice of his suddenly sounded gentle and swaying as I remembered what had happened. Or had it all been a bad dream? It most certainly didn't feel like it.

"Good morning, my soet Ivy," he greeted me as I felt him gently brush my cheek. I stayed as still as a board, keeping my eyes on the ceiling with the fancy canned lightings that were nothing like I had ever seen. The lights were bright, letting me know that I wasn't at my apartment and I wasn't at a hospital. It looked too fancy.

I opened my mouth to speak, but nothing came out. Instead, I tried to feel whatever pain he had put me through. I kept praying that it had been a bad dream and the reason that I was lying beside him now is that I somehow lost consciousness the moment I opened the door and he brought me to wherever this is. I tried to feel my right hand, but I couldn't even wiggle my fingers, not from pain, but from a certain numbness that made my right hand feel as if it were the size of big air balloon. My right ear felt the exact same way, and it made me feel dizzy, but also a bit delirious, like all I wanted to do was giggle at the strange feeling. I felt like I would float away.

I gasped, "don't let me float away," I rushed out to say suddenly, my voice croaking out with a hoarseness that scratched at my throat.

He chuckled, "and let you get away from me? Never." He answered me, however I refused to face him. "Did you like my lullaby? I know you don't understand Afrikaans but it was the Brahms Lullaby. Ma used to sing it to me every night, and I guess watching you sleep made me want to sing it for you until you woke up." He pressed a kiss to my dry and chapped lips, "you're so beautiful..." he croaked out, his face now hovering over mine, blocking my view of the ceiling that I had been finding entertaining ever since I woke up.

I looked into those blue eyes of his that shined down on me with admiration that was suffocating. It made me feel shy, he made me feel like I was the Mona Lisa, and like I was art he could spend an eternity studying. God, I couldn't breathe. My lungs filled up with air, but the way that he peered down at me as if he were willing to suck every bit of it into his, filling himself with me; made me feel like whatever he felt for me; it would last forever.

I swallowed, "wha…what happened?" I found myself asking, needing to break him away from looking at me and admiring me.

He smirked, his smirk dark and ominous as if he knew exactly what I was thinking. "It definitely wasn't a dream," he began, running his tongue along his bottom lip, "but, guess what?" his smirk turned into a grin that only portrayed an excitement that only a child could have. It caused goosebumps to rise on my arms as my eyes widened and my heart skipped a beat.

"Wh…at?" I let out in a horrified whisper about what he was about to tell me. The man was deranged and I wanted nothing more than to get as far away from him as possible.

"We're twinning," he said with a chuckle. "See," he seemed to go into an explanation, "after you passed out from me slicing your ear off, I thought to myself, 'hm, what should I do with this ear?' and then, and then," he seemed to get excited, leaning down and taking a big whiff of my scent as if it were a drug he couldn't get enough of, "I thought, 'yes…my, why don't I just keep it all to myself. For the rest of my life. For eternity.' And then, I took that little blade that still had your blood on it, and got to cut my own ear off. I sliced that motherfucker right off, and then I called my surgeon and told him to take your precious ear and attach it to mine, and take mine…" he created some distance between us and then turned his head sideways, showing me his ear, "and attach it to yours."

My eyes widened to the size of saucers as I looked at his right ear, finding my very ear stitched and stapled to the jagged lower half of his ear. The stark contrast between our two skin tones made it obvious that it wasn't his ear, and I let out a shocked gasp at the sight that met me because it was unlike anything I had ever seen before.

He still had that excited grin on his face, "do you like it?" he chuckled deeply, "Sakkie thought you would, he said it would be romantic. Ruan wanted to eat it and Botha wanted me to turn into a necklace for you to learn your lesson. I guess this time, Sakkie won." What the fuck? "Here, see yours," he pulled a hand mirror from behind him and then held it above my face and I turned my head sideways and lo and behold I had a pale ivory ear attached to the jagged lower half of my honey toned ear.

My jaw dropped and my left hand covered my gapping mouth as I stared into the mirror like this was some kind of hoax. It had to be some terrible, twisted joke. I couldn't have had my ear sliced off and replaced with a white man's ear, I refused to believe it. I had to have been dreaming, but I knew I wasn't. With each passing moment as I looked at my ear, things seemed to get more and more dangerous as I tried to wrap my head around how sick of a man Schalk was.

"Wha...what the...fu-he-...what?" I stammered in confusion, my voice coming out in a horrified whisper as I looked away from the mirror and the excited grin on his face as he looked back at me. My stomach churned and my heart raced, "you...y...wh...no...I-m-k..." I couldn't find the words as I looked at him like I couldn't seem to understand how he could be so...him.

"You're mine, Ivy. Ours, you're ours," he added, setting the mirror down and then caging me in his arms as he hovered over me. "You're all ours, and now you know it. You'll have a piece of me for the rest of your life and I'll have a piece of you for the rest of mine." He leaned down and captured my lips in his and even though all I wanted to do was shove him off and kill him, I let him kiss me and returned the kiss, crying. He moved his lips expertly through my own unlike any other man that I have ever kissed. It made my toes curl and it made my brain cells suddenly become inactive at the way that he moved them as if kissing me was what he was born to do. Such contradictory emotions, I couldn't explain it. He parted our lips after some time, placing a few pecks as we slowed down. "You did so well, babygirl," he purred against my lips, his voice merely above a whisper, "you took your punishment like the good girl I know you are..." his voice sounded sinfully erotic even to my horrified ears. He praised me like I wanted his approval, and at this point, I'd do anything to keep him happy. I needed to get out of here, and if being a good girl was what he wanted, then I'd be it.

"Good girls get rewarded," his eyes stayed on mine as he said this, before he dipped his head down my neck and pressed his lips to the sensitive skin of my neck. My tears were still flowing down my face, into my ears and onto the pillow that I was laying on.

I wanted to bite my bottom lip but it still hurt so I opted on just gritting my teeth as I felt him slide his body under the blanket with me, and then his right hand moved down my body. I realised then, that I was dressed in something short, a short dress...nightgown...hospital gown, maybe? It was short and light. I felt every bit of his caresses as his hand moved down my body, making its way between my thighs as I sucked in a breath and shut my eyes.

His head and lips dipped lower and lower, his teeth bit and sucked on the flesh that he passed and I knew that they would leave a mark. I clenched my hands into fists as I attempted to grit my teeth so hard, I feared they would shatter. I didn't want him to hear the effect that he had on my body, but the moment that he managed to dip his head between my breasts, and then capture my left nipple between his lips, short breaths of measured pleasure escaped me.

"There we go," he purred as if that was the reaction that he wanted. I felt his fingers dance against my clit, soliciting a moan that I hadn't known would escape to permeate through the air as he continued to suck on my nipple and play with my clit. His teeth began to bite and softly nibble on my nipple, and his thumb circled my clit, while his fingers worked at my entrance, causing more and more wetness. I was easily aroused, that, I knew.

I had a few make out sessions before with two different boyfriends that I've had, but it was innocent. I was a church girl especially when I lived with Kuku, so I only dated church boys, and the furthest I went was probably second base. I have never let a man touch what lay between my legs. I planned for that to be a privilege only my husband would partake in.

I felt him line a finger to my entrance and my thighs quivered in anticipation as he pulled his face away from my breasts and looked down at my face as if he wanted to commit the memory of my first intrusion to memory. I wanted to look away from his gaze, but his eyes compelled me to stay on his as I felt him squeeze two fingers into me. I grimaced, feeling the strange intrusion and I let out an uncomfortable moan at the foreign and painful feeling as he smiled.

"Fuck, you're tight," he groaned as he shoved his fingers deep inside me and my left hand rushed to grip his wrist, pleading for him to be gentle since it hurt.

"It-t hu-hurts," I said in a grunt, pleading with my eyes for him to stop or go slower but he glared down at me.

"You're not trying to stop me, are you, my Ivy?" he asked me, pulling his fingers all the way out of my hole. I immediately shook my head, removing my hand from his wrist, "because that wouldn't be very good girl of you," he shoved his fingers back inside me and I let out a choked scream, throwing my head back at the intrusion that was anything but gentle as he continued to pull his fingers all the way out, and then shove them all the way in, and I grabbed a fistful of sheets in my left fist– unable to move my right one. Gradually, the pain began to subside and then pleasure overtook me, pain and pleasure worked hand in hand and then I let out uncontrollable moans as my legs opened wider and his fingers made work of my insides. He twisted his fingers inside me, bending them and causing his knuckles to brush against my walls as my back arched.

"F-f...fuck," I let out in a long moan as I felt my walls and stomach tighten and a sensation unlike any other washed over me in waves. I lifted my back off the bed, feeling my eyes roll to the back of my head and my breath catch at the back of my throat. For a second, I saw stars and my vision was black.

I struggled to catch my breath as my thighs quivered uncontrollably from the over stimulation and the great level of pleasure, "look at you," he purred as he tilting my head upward, making me open my eyes and look at him. He lifted his right hand, covered in my juices and I felt my face flush at the mess that I had made all over his hand, "so much fucking cream," he brought his fingers to his mouth, sucking them off as if they were the best flavoured thing he could ever get his hands on. He slurped on it, taking all of my juices as if it were his only sustenance.

I turned my head to look away from him only for him to make me look back at him, "ask me where I'm going now." He instructed me as he bent down and gave me a toe curling kiss that had my eyes rolling to the back of my head.

I tried to catch my breath, or even come down from the high that I had experienced, "where...where are you going now?" I asked him, my voice coming out small and strained.

"You remember Benjamin, or should I say, Benny?" he asked me, his eyes no longer clouded with lust and I felt the hairs on the back of my neck stand at the mention of the name that had made all of this happen. Every bit of ecstasy that I had been feeling went away and I was as awake and terrified as I had been minutes prior. I found myself nodding, "I'm going to kill him, and I'm going to bring him back here and put him right over there," he gestured to the corner in the room and then looked back at me, "and then I'm going to fuck you while his body sits there and rots."

Chapter 9

I took in a deep breath, sitting on the hood of the open-sided camouflage Toyota Land Cruiser with a sun canopy, while I enjoyed the rays of the harsh sun on my exposed skin.

"Damn, mosquitoes," my father complained as he slapped at his thigh, where a mosquito had probably been feasting on his skin as we sat side by side, father and son.

It was peaceful between the two of us as I sat with the rifle between my legs, a long straw between my teeth and a camouflage hat on my head to shield me from the sun rays. My father was dressed the same as I was as he drank a silver flask of Hennessy like it was nothing, looking out at the massive farm that he had.

"I thought mosquitoes only come out at night," I added, thinking a bit, as I creased my eyebrows and tilted my head in his direction and looked at him.

He shrugged, like he wasn't sure and he couldn't care less, "well, something was biting me and whatever it was; fuck it."

We both chuckled, and then he rolled his eyes as we heard the screams, "shut up!" he yelled back at the man who was struggling to crawl away from the cackle of hyenas that had spotted him, and were now making their way towards him. Pa turned to regard me, "you know, you didn't have to shoot the boy in the kneecaps the moment he started running," my father said with a smile as he reached for his own rifle that he had placed across his lap. "He's been crawling for over half an hour now."

Pa was an impatient man, I had promised him blood and a show, and at this point he was just dying for one. I placed my fingers in my mouth and whistled loudly for my pets to be drawn towards us. The hyenas perked up at the sound of my whistle and their deranged laughs made their way to my ears as I watched Benjamin claw his fingers into the dirt, pleading for me to help him as he attempted to crawl even further away but he was badly wounded, and losing a lot of blood. He had been in the sun for 45 minutes now and his strength was quickly depleting. On top of that, he was dehydrated and starved because I had kept him locked up since yesterday.

"Finally," pa bellowed with a proud clap as he watched the hyenas run towards my whistle.

"No! Please!" Benjamin yelled, turning his head in our direction. "Please, Mr du Toit! I'm sorry! No!" he shouted fearfully, his eyes wide with fear as the first hyena reached him, a female. She didn't care to inspect him, she immediately tore her teeth into his leg, ripping at it, swishing her head side to side, and the others rushed to join her, knowing that if they took too long then they wouldn't get any more of this delicious meal.

My father sighed, almost sadly, "I'm actually going to miss him. He spoke really good Afrikaans. It's hard to find his kind that's actually good with the boer tongue," my father tusked, shaking his head as we watched Benjamin scream bloody murder as the hyenas tugged and fought over him; eating him alive.

The sight was ghastly but it pleased me, it felt good to watch it all go down. I would have done it myself but there was a reason that I called pa and Johannes here, this discussion needed my full attention, and besides, I hadn't fed my beloved pets for about three days now, so they were starved and ready, savage and desperate and it was pleasing to hear the now gargled sounds of Benjamin.

We heard the sound of tyres on the dirt, making their way towards us and we looked towards the other Land Cruiser, identical to ours, and my brother, Johannes was behind the wheel as he parked the car right beside us. He jumped out of the car dressed in a suit that was slightly dishevelled, his jacket nowhere in sight but his white dress shirt deeply stained in crimson, as he opened the back door of the Land Cruiser and pulled out a limp body. He pulled out the body of his girlfriend that looked like she had been taught a lesson and didn't pass the test. He threw her over his shoulder and then walked past us, dumping her body a few feet away, not too close to the hyenas since they didn't like him all that much but far enough from us so that they wouldn't be sniffing at our feet.

He then made his way towards us, "she's broken," he said with a head shake of disappointment and I knew the feeling of a broken toy, it was sad but satisfying. She had lasted a long time, I thought that she could possibly be the one that he would call his, but no, turns out she's as weak as all the others.

I held out my hand to help him hop onto the hood of the car and join pa and I. Johannes sat on the left side of me while pa sat on my right. He placed a hand on my shoulder, looking at the scene of the hyenas tearing up his girlfriend now, eagerly dipping their teeth into fresh meat, "so what did you want to talk about, broer (brother)?" he asked me in English and pa and I rolled our eyes and groaned at the fact that he spoke that darned language. If it wasn't my darling Ivy speaking it, I didn't want to hear that shit.

He chuckled, obviously enjoying how it made us angry before swiftly changing back to Afrikaans and repeating the question. We sat in silence for a bit, both of them waiting for me to answer, "Pa, Johannes," I took a steadying breath, feeling myself get nervous.

Oh my God! This is actually happening! Sakkie squealed in my head, sounding exactly like the pussy we peg him to be.

What...what the fuck was that? Botha grunted out in the same shock that we were all experiencing.

No, somebody's got to kill Sakkie. There's no other fucking way. What the fuck was that shit? Did he just fucking squeal?! Get this pussy away from us, Schalk. This is the final straw! Ruan raged, his voice coming out thick with disgust at Sakkie and his squealing.

"I've called you both here for a very serious conversation. One that I didn't think I'd ever be having, yet, here I am," we weren't a close knit family. We didn't eat breakfast together, or have Sunday lunches as a family. Especially now that Johannes and I had our own places, and were adults leading our own lives. We met up every now and then, sending random texts here and there, meeting at work as if we were strangers. It was who the du Toit's were, but it didn't mean that we weren't united. If there was any kind of emergency, we were all there. Just as it was when we were kids, pa was the protective figure that fathers were and ma worried too much about our health and whether we'd eaten or not. "I've found a very special woman, special, like ma is to pa," I said slowly, letting the words sink in between the empty spaces. "I want to make her mine. I want to marry her," I turned to face pa, watching his eyes widen in surprise at what I was saying, "I want to get married, pa."

You could hear a pin drop in the silence that enveloped us. It was no secret that I wasn't the son that pa expected this from, hell, I hadn't even expected it from myself. I expected this from Johannes, and so did pa, and ma, and ouma, and oupa, and Pieter. Johannes was the girlfriend type. Johannes cared to find a nice girl, spoil her, and teach her lessons only when it was necessary, but he was the more perfect son. He was social, the best kind of son there was, women loved him, he wore suits and ties, and was only chauffeured around, and he drank whisky, and played golf as if he were born on a golf course. Johannes was the type to settle down, while I enjoyed the life of a bachelor. I did what I wanted, when I wanted. I owned a penthouse, crashed every sports car that I had because of my reckless driving, partied with a new girl on my arm every night, I played with them, took them back to my place, only to have them running down the streets of Sandton, bloodied and limping in fear, while I lurk in the shadows and strike again when they think that they're safe. I hated golf, but loved rugby, I spent my free time with my hyenas, and I got drunk off of Corona. I was hot headed and hard headed, and I could sit in a meeting, and if someone even looks at me the wrong way, I'd put a bullet between their eyes; it's happened before. My work days were when I preferred them to be, and I didn't shit around when it came to my personal space.

"I'm guessing that's whose ear that is," pa gestured to my new addition and I smiled, nodding my head. He chuckled before throwing his arm over my shoulder and pulling me into a side hug. "This is great news, son, ma will be happy. Very happy, you know she's always wanted a daughter in law...and grandkids, lots of them," he said with a suggestive hint while hitting my shoulder with a punch.

We laughed and I nodded my head before Johannes spoke up, "damn," he chuckled with a scoff, "who would've thought someday you'd be talking about wanting to marry a kaffir," he commented, and I nodded my head at the comment. It was true, we came from a long line of pure Afrikaner, and I was proud of it. We didn't mix at all with black people, not even in the least bit, except if they were our workers, then sure, but never in our personal circles. It was almost unheard of, for a Du Toit to be with a black person and I'm sure that this is history in the making. Hell, if you would have told me a month ago, I'd be talking about marrying a black woman, I'd have shot you between the eyes. My hatred, dislike, and disgust towards them ran deep through my veins, except when it came to her, then it all fell away.

It didn't mean that I was suddenly all kumbaya about kaffirs, but my Ivy was different. She was my Ivy, she was perfect. She was above the rest of them, different, and that's why I was going to marry her.

"Call her that again, and I'll strip you naked and have my pets eat your fucking cock for breakfast, you hear me?" I asked him, raising an eyebrow and grinning. He laughed, ruffling my hair in a way that I absolutely despised but he still did because he was 'older'. Siblings, I tell you, they don't get any less annoying when they're 34 years old.

"So what's the plan?" Johannes asked me and I put my fingers to my lips, whistling again for the hyenas to get going. They stood at attention and then all scurried off, leaving behind the remains of Johannes' girlfriend and Benjamin.

"Well, she's black, and you know how they have all that lobola (bride price) business, so I'm thinking I get in touch with her family. I want to sort it out, quick, and then I'd like for our wedding to be at most, two months from now, because I plan on getting her pregnant as soon as in half an hour. So I think she should have the wedding of her dreams just before her belly starts showing," I had already thought it all through. I planned to give my Ivy all that she has ever dreamed of, every car, every house, every clothing, everything. I was going to give it to her. At the moment, I was waiting for her custom Brabus G63 to arrive so I could chuck that Datsun Go in the rubbish where it belongs.

"I'm glad to hear that you want to slow down and start a family, Schalk. I'm going to support you. You also know that this means, the family business has to change, right?" Johannes and I nodded as pa spoke. "I've been building those offices in Cape Town for the past 7 months, they're going to be ready as soon as next month. So, Schalk and Johannes, you're both going to have to sit down and decide where you would prefer to head. One of you will have to stay in Sandton and the other will have to go to Cape Town to head the new offices, so I'll leave it to the two of you."

Johannes and I faced each other, silent, as if communicating through our eyes. I knew that he was saying that he was fine with whichever decision I make. I nodded my head, "let me discuss with Ivy first, and then I'll get back to you." He agreed with a curt nod.

"We can definitely go more in depth with that once you two have reached a mutual decision. But until then, Schalk, I'm excited to be a great parent. Johannes...look at your younger brother already getting married, and you're still breaking your toys," my father tusked in the disappointment that was usually directed at me.

Johannes laughed, "my, how the tables have turned," he and I shared a hearty laugh as I set the rifle down behind me and then hopped down from the hood of the car.

"You planning on taking her back to her family?" I asked Johannes as he also hopped down from the hood, walking towards me as we observed the nearly only-bone remains of his ex-girlfriend.

He was silent for a bit, in thought, "yeah, I guess so. They deserve closure."

"What story are you going to come up with this one?" this wasn't the first time that Johannes had killed one of his women. The pathetic thing was the way that he attempted to cover it up. He always cared too damn much about giving families closure. Fuck that, next time teach your daughter to not be so fucking naïve and be fooled by men like us.

"Hunting trip gone wrong," he shrugged, "I'm going to make sure I get a couple of scratches and bruises to sell the story. She got mauled by a puma, or something like that. It happens, you know?" he asked me as I ignored him, shaking my head and walking over to Benjamin's mauled body that had chunks ripped off of it and blood pooled all over the dried grass as I picked up his half eaten body and dragged it back to the Land Cruiser.

Pa jumped into the one that Johannes arrived in, "I'm leaving you fucks behind. I need to take a shit!" he exclaimed over the sound of the engine as he left Johannes and I to clean up our mess.

Chapter 10

D^{o I?}
      Don't I?
   Do I?
   Don't I?
   ...Do I?

I sat on the edge of the bed, my wide and fearful eyes stuck on the door handle that led out of this room. My heart raced in anticipation, and my body trembled in fear of the thoughts that I was having. Schalk had been gone for some time, and in that time, I fought against whether to up and run, or to stay here. I didn't know what he had in store for me, and I didn't want to find out, but when it came to Schalk my wants meant nothing. Only his. I knew that once he walked through that door again, more trauma would come to me. And I also knew that if I got up and ran, far worse trauma would come to me.

   ...I don't.

This was Schalk's home and there was no way that he didn't know the workings in and out of this place. If I tried to run, he'd surely find me. It would be so easy for him too. What if it was a test, a trap? What if he was testing me, to see if given the opportunity, would I try to leave him? Schalk's a deranged man, he could, and would do anything to hurt me to prove that he loves me, or that I'm his. I don't believe that the man loves me, I think I've become some sick part in his game. I wonder how many other women he's done this to.

I didn't want to think about how he would drag Benny in here...what condition Benny would be in...

Oh God...

I do, I decided on a whim, shooting up from the edge of the bed with the speed of lightning as I ran straight for the door. My body sluggishly collided with the door because I was dizzy, "oh no..." I sighed, gripping onto the expensive feeling wood of the door, my hands dancing along it to find the door handle as I closed my eyes, blinking several times to try and restore my balance. I found the door handle with my left hand and immediately tugged on it, and it moved, opening the door easily.

I didn't know if that was a good or bad thing, that the door wasn't locked. It either meant that this was indeed a test or trap, or it could mean that he was so confident that I wouldn't find my way out of here. Either way, I didn't stay to think about it. I blinked, hoping that with each second that my eyes were covered in darkness, it would stop the spinning of the world around me.

I tripped over my own feet, gripping onto the walls, as I let out panicked breaths, trying to run. It felt like it did in horror movies, when the girl is running and stumbling, breathing heavy, terrified, and you know that the killer is lurking somewhere in the shadows and you just want her to hurry up and get to safety. It had that sense of foreboding.

I kept looking over my shoulder, feeling tears escape my eyes as my legs felt like they weighed a ton, but I didn't care. I kept pushing myself to run even further, get as far away from here as possible. As I reached the middle of the long hallway with a few doors lined on each wall, I was greeted with a staircase. A drunken smile spread across my face as I rushed to it, grabbing onto the black railings along the stairs and gripping onto them as I attempted to make my way down-stairs. I had counted four stairs that I was able to make my way down, but due to my haste and delirious state, my feet tripped and I went down. I tumbled, letting out a surprised shout as I felt myself roll down uncontrollably until I reached the bottom and ended up on my face. I began to cry, raising my head from the floor after a prolonged moment of silence. I looked around me, praying that I wouldn't lift my head and find Schalk standing in front of me, looking down on me with his dark blue eyes.

I tried to sit up, but it hurt too badly. I let out pained grunts as I used my hands to drag my weight, along the ceramic tiled floors. My right hand was bandaged, the bandages had become bloody around my palm, reminding me of Schalk and how he had stabbed me with the glass. I cried even more, but grit my teeth, using my left hand to pull most of my weight, as I looked around frantically, looking for a door.

My answer seemed to come then, when a person suddenly walked into my line of view. My eyes were wide as I set them on the familiar built body that belonged to my boss, Mr Bertus du Toit. He stood several metres away, dressed in a pair of camouflage shorts, and a matching shirt that had been tucked in. His muscles showed through the shirt, and his dark hair had more than a few grey hairs. Mr Bertus was no ugly looking man, he had the sort of appeal that older men did. He was a man of money, a man of wealth and success and he carried on like that. He walked with his head high, his stride was confident, his eyes were cold, and he wore expensive suits and Rolex watches. He yelled at whoever dared to meet his eyes, and at the moment, he was looking right at me. I couldn't tell what he was thinking, since he was far away and the world was still spinning around me, "Mr Bertus..." I let out in a pained grunt, my cries becoming louder because I was sure that Schalk's father would help me.

"Please...help me," I begged, looking behind me and then dragging myself towards him. "Schalk, he, he," I stammered over my words, feeling my stomach churn in the fear of Schalk appearing at any moment and dismissing me in front of his father. But I could only pray that Mr Bertus would get me out of here. He doesn't even have to punish his son, as long as he just lets me leave, that's all I want. I figure he won't do anything to Schalk, but I just need him to get me into a car and get me out of here, and I won't ever have to see any of them again. After this, my ass is leaving Gauteng, and I'm booking it to Lesotho or Botswana. "He's hurt me, and he, he cut my ear, and cut his own. He...He's crazy. Please help me, before he sees me," I pleaded with him, my words desperate and fast, stumbling over one another as I watched as Mr Bertus strode towards me, covering majority of the distance as I struggled to crawl out of there.

I stopped struggling when Mr Bertus stopped in front of me. I lifted my head, craning my neck as I peered up at him with blurry eyes and uncoordinated eye sight. I watched as he crouched down onto his knee in front of me. He was silent, while I cried, mumbling several 'please' with wet lips and chattering teeth. He reached out a hand and gently brushed his fingers along my face, "you're bleeding," he finally croaked out in that powerful voice of his that suddenly reminded me so much of his son.

I blinked, nodding my head. "I f-fell down the stairs," I chose to explain, "Please, Mr Bertus, please, help me." I gripped onto his ankle, my fingers wrapping around it in a death grip as I plead as if I was a moment's away from death. In which I was. "He can't-can't find me. Schalk...he's obsessed with me. He broke into m-my house, he-he stabbed my palm and cut half of my ea-ear off. Please, Mr Bertus, he's going to-to kill me!"

He watched me, silent and then leaned in, covering the distance between us. I watched as he moved his face beside mine, bringing his lips to my right ear, "I can only hope." He finally said, his words coming out cold and spine chilling. I felt my fingers grip around his ankles tighten from the fear that his words instilled in me, and his cold tone that felt like he was taking joy in all of this. "My son isn't crazy, miss Ivy, how dare you insult my creation?"

He moved away from my ear and finally brought his face in front of my own, his blue eyes reminding me so much of the man that I had been running away from. In that moment, I saw the same look in his eyes as I had seen in Schalk, there was a craziness in there that one couldn't shake. My jaw went slack as I let his words wash over, and he seemed to drink in my appearance.

"Pa– oh, I see you're already bonding with your daughter in law," Schalk's voice cut through the silence as he strode into the room, and I wasn't able to understand what he was saying. Schalk was dressed like his father, except he held two large buckets in each of his hands, and blood dripped from the buckets, onto the floor. However, I hadn't seen that due to my poor eyesight at that moment.

Mr Bertus turned and faced his son, standing to his feet, "they're always a lot more fun before they're broken, son." Mr Bertus faced me again, moving his leg away from me but my fingers wrapped around it even tighter.

"No! Please! Don't let him take me!" I began to shout, pleading with Mr Bertus even though it was obvious that he wasn't going to help me. At this point, anything was better than the man who had now covered the distance and was standing beside his father.

"She was trying to escape. She fell down the stairs and that's why she's bleeding. I don't want you accusing me of touching her. She's yours to hurt. I've got your mother."

Mr Bertus continued speaking to his son and ignoring my desperate please.

"Mr Bertus, please! I swear, I-I won't tell an-anyone what happened! I swear." I continued, crying over whatever their conversation was.

"I figured she'd try to run, I thought she would've left a lot earlier, but I'm glad she didn't. It seems like I won't have to break her for much longer before she's exactly how I want her." Schalk began to chuckle, "I wonder how she would've dealt with my pets."

His father laughed, "And they're right outside the door. You need to put leashes on those fucking things, they're fucking up your mum's garden, and they keep digging up the graves of all of your favourite toys."

"Did Ma invite Pieter for Sunday supper?" Schalk continued with his father.

"Mr Bertus, please! He's going to hurt me! Please! He's a monster!"

It was like I wasn't even there, as they continued to converse, "She did. Why? Do you want to tell them about the bride to be?" Mr Bertus responded.

Schalk nodded, "yes, I do." Schalk looked down at me and my eyes met his, he set the buckets down and then crouched down to my level. He was silent, his eyes washing over every part of my face as if drinking me in for the first time, "Why don't you let my father go, my soet Ivy? We've got plans, remember?" he asked me, tilting his head to the side with a smile on his face as I began to cry. My cries came out broken and panicked.

"Sch-Schalk...please...I'm sorry," I began to plead in whispered sobs.

"Let him go, and don't make me repeat myself," he said as he stood to his feet and then faced his father.

"Your mother's going to be really happy that you're spending the night over, especially with her." Mr Bertus nodded his head at me, "she'll want to know every little thing about her future daughter."

"I've got plans for tomorrow so I'm going to leave early in the morning tomorrow. But, ma won't see her tonight, she'll see her during breakfast. With what I have planned for my Ivy, she'll be using a wheelchair tomorrow." I found myself letting go of Mr Bertus' leg. I cried as I watched Schalk reach out for me. He easily lifted me into his arms, and then threw me over his shoulder. My arms swung below me, and my head spun what felt like a million kilometres a minute, and I groaned at the feeling. I shut my eyes, trying to still the busy world as Schalk easily lifted the two buckets into his hands and made his way back the very way that I had just come.

"...no..." I let out in a horrified whisper, thinking about what he said he was going to do to me. He walked up the stairs and then made his way into that room again. We entered it and he closed the door behind him. Schalk set the buckets down and then walked over to the bed and set me on it gently. I landed with a soft bounce as I shut my eyes, groaning as I touched my head at the amount of pain that I was feeling at the moment.

I opened my eyes after a moment, hearing the sound of the buckets and then looked at Schalk. I watched as he walked over to the corner that he'd pointed that he'd put Benny at. I suddenly felt my stomach churn as I watched him pick up one of the buckets and tip it over, dropping the remains of what I was sure was Benny. I let out a horrified screech, my eyes widening to saucers as a head fell out and dirty blood fell out onto the pristine floors. Schalk was unmoved by the sounds that I made and reached for the second bucket, doing the same and revealing a mangled corpse, and insides that obviously had been eaten at and now only a few remained.

"Damn," Schalk swore as he reached into the pile of Benny's remains and pulled out the head from under the pile and set it perfectly on top of the pile. He stepped back and looked at it, "perfect." He said.

The stench from Benny's remains clogged into every orifice I had and I couldn't help it as I threw my body over the side of the bed, away from it, and vomited because of the sickening smell. "Now," Schalk spoke over the sound of my vomiting, "my soet Ivy, this, this...this is going to be fun." He said with a chuckle, turning away from the pile and stripping himself of his shirt, his dark blue eyes turning a sinister black. I crawled further onto the bed, shaking my head side to side as I watched him cover the distance between us. "You ought to be afraid, Ivy..." he said in a whisper as he rested his bloody hands on the bed, leaning over it to get to my legs, his fingers wrapping around my ankles and dragging my body towards him, "I bite."

Chapter 11

Gag noises echoed through the room as Schalk gripped onto my hair, pressing my face into his pelvis as he pounded his member deep inside my throat, cutting off my air supply and making me pound my desperate fists against his thighs. My ears were ringing, my head felt like it was going to explode, and my pussy was sensitive and hurt from what had to have been hours of him fingering me and eating me out like he'd never get the chance again.

Schalk had my face trapped between his thighs, his balls hitting against my chin as my eyes rolled to the back of my head. My legs were kicking every which way, attempting to fight for the breath that he wouldn't let me have. He had been shoving his cock so deep down my throat, that I was sure my jaw was broken at this point because it's never been open this wide, for this long. I felt the already iron drip in my hair become even more ferocious before I heard Schalk let out a series of cuss words and thrust down my throat one last time, staying in place as I felt him twitch above me, and a warm liquid moved down my throat.

He slowly pulled himself out of my mouth, his long member seeming to take an eternity, and as soon as I felt him pulling out, I rushed away from him, screaming, "p-please!" I cried, coughing and heaving. The tears that slid down my cheeks had wet my chin, breasts, and even stomach. I was swimming in my own tears as I looked at him with frightened eyes because he was so sinister, "en-enough, pl-please!" I begged, sobbing and praying that was all that he wanted to do.

Schalk sat on his knees, his left hand going through his now sweaty and messy hair while the right hand was wrapped around his member that was slick with my saliva. I looked to the large meat between his legs; the pink bulbous and angry head, the way his member stood erect, hitting against his lower stomach; it looked like it was going to hurt, a lot. "I haven't even gotten to fucking you yet, Ivy." He said with a dry chuckle, running his thumb across the tip of his member and then letting out a soft sigh, his now black eyes looking over every inch of my naked body, "come here, babygirl," he called to me, stretching his left hand towards me as I began to shake my head and cry.

"It's-It's too big, pl-please," I cried, pleading with him to not do what he had promised me he would. He was unmoved, his black eyes showed his lust for me. They seemed to be more focused on my naked breasts and the hard nipples, with the drops of blood from how hard he had been sucking. My breasts still hurt from how hard he had slapped them, tugged on them and bit them. They were covered in dark bites, some even with blood from how hard he had bitten me. "Schalk please!" I continued to sob, watching his figure through blurry tears. He hadn't said anything and I knew that meant that he expected me to do as he says, "please, Schalk, pl-please!" I continued to plead, even though I pulled my body away from the headboard, slowly making my way towards his hand.

My hand was taking an eternity to reach his, but when my own left hand was placed in his larger one, his fingers curled around my hand and then tugged hard, pulling me closer to him. I let out a gasp as he pulled me into his body and then placed his lips on mine, kissing me until I began to moan in his mouth. I felt him rub the tip of the head on my clit, since my legs were open as I stood before him on my knees as well. He wrapped his left hand around my waist, his hand making its way to my ass that he grabbed a handful off before slapping it, and I jumped from the painful action.

His lips left my own as they made their way to my neck, biting and sucking as I let out both pained and pleasure filled moans. He slowly pushed his body on mine, causing mine to fall back; making my back meet with the mattress. He set his knee between my legs because the first thing I tried to do was close them, but he was ahead of the action. His hands made work of spreading my legs wide, creating enough room for his large body to fit in between them. I began to struggle against him, "Schalk...please, please, I'm begging you. Don't do this," I continued to cry as his hands were on my thighs, pressing them down onto the bed and forcing them wide open.

His eyes were drawn towards my gaping womanhood as if he could spend an eternity looking at it. I didn't know what was making me sicker, Benny's disgusting remains just a few feet away with his severed and badly wounded face looking in my direction, or the look of pure hunger in Schalk's eyes as he looked down at me like he couldn't wait to fuck me. My chest moved up and down rapidly as I watched him bring his hips closer to mine. I looked to the large member that was drawing closer to my most intimate and vulnerable part, and I began to fight. I slapped his chest, trying to do anything that would get him away from me, but it didn't work.

He suddenly gripped either side of my cheeks, causing my lips to pucker up and my frightened eyes to meet his own dark ones, "look at me, babygirl, fucking look at me," he snapped, his voice thick with lust and a cockiness that made me sick to my stomach. My teary eyes peered into his, "this is my fucking pussy, do you hear me?" I felt his tip at my entrance, "I'll fuck it whenever I want. I don't need your fucking permission to do what I want with what I own," his words were cold and the grip of possessiveness in them towards me made my body rigid as stone, but that wasn't for long because he suddenly pounded into me and I let out a scream at the sudden intrusion.

My head flew back, my hands gripped onto his shoulders, and my nails dug into his back and drew blood as he continued to thrust into me, "that's it, babygirl," he growled into my ear, his hands holding my thighs down and spreading me even further if that was possible. "Squeeze daddy's dick, just like that," his words in my ear were sinful, dirty, nasty, derogative– and my nipples hardened at them. The sound of skin slapping against skin filled the room, and my screams turned to those of pain and pleasure, a combination that made me want to run away from him, but also pull him closer to me.

His thrusts were merciless. My breasts bounced with each pound, and his cock was so big it was stretching me whole, and going so deep that it hurt to the point of insanity. The tears continued to escape me as I lifted my head, my eyes connecting with his that looked down at me with a prowl of a lion to its prey, as if soaking in the sight of me weak beneath him. His body towered over mine, his face that of perfection even in a moment like this. I threw my head back and moaned, unable to fight the orgasm that came quick, "f-fuck!" I let out in between body tremors as he continued to thrust into me even during my orgasm.

He pulled my body up, and then flipped me over, bringing his hand under my stomach and putting my butt in the air, all the while, not slipping out of me. "Sc-Schalk!" I screamed at the painful feeling of this position. All I could say, was that it burned, like hell. His pounds felt more merciless and quick, forceful and precise, always going deeper and deeper. I gripped the sheets with desperate fists, as he pressed his hand into the back of my head and shoved my face into the bed. His other hand was gripping my boobs, slapping them, tugging on them and pulling on the nipples so hard, I thought he wanted to pull them off.

"Sch-Scha– pl-please!" I cried incoherently, trying to struggle against him but I felt weak and powerless under him. My words were an unintelligible mess.

Schalk brought his hand across my ass, slapping it so hard, I let out a hoarse scream, and he repeated the action again, and again, and it felt like my ass was going to fall off as I started to fight against him, "say my name, Ivy," he growled out, and I knew he was in the throes of pleasure at the moment.

"Schalk!" I let out in a quick and desperate shout, quick to appease him and make him hear whatever he wanted, "Schalk..." I let out in a cry as I felt him slap my ass again, this time even harder than the other times, making me feel like I wouldn't get the chance to sit on my ass again after this.

"That's not my name. Say my name, my Ivy. Make me happy," he slapped my clit this time, wrapping his index and thumb around the nub and pulling on it until it felt like he was going to rip it off at any moment. I tried to close my legs, but his body was between my legs and he had me in such a position that I was vulnerable to him and his ongoing assault.

I felt my stomach churn, my insides squeeze and my body seemed to go into sudden overdrive, "da-...daddy!" I let out in a loud and deep moan as I felt a second orgasm wash over me in waves, "daddy," I said again, deep in the throes of ecstasy as I felt his balls slap against my sensitive and wounded clit.

"N-n-no, Schalk, pl-plea-please!" I let out in a hoarse whisper as I felt him push my body into further into the mattress using his own body. His front was to my back, his body crushing mine under his as I began to fight under the crushing weight of his body. His member slipped out of me and he leaned into my ear, his right hand reaching around my neck, cutting off my air supply.

"Put me back inside, babygirl," he whispered softly in my ear, his lips brushing against the very ear that he had hurt. I bit my lip, crying softly as I did as he said. I reached between us, reached between my legs and searched for his member. My hands were shaking as I gripped it and brought it to my overly sensitive lips.

"Schalk...please..." I pleaded one last time, my voice coming out raspy and broken. "It's too much, it's too much," I cried, because each time I brought his tip closer to my pussy, the overly sensitive entrance made me hiss.

His hand wrapped tighter around my neck, keeping me in place, making it harder for me to breathe, "you're not trying to stop me from taking what's mine, are you, soet Ivy?" he asked me, his voice becoming a deadly whisper as if the horrors that would await me for not letting him fuck my already raw pussy to the point of non-existence would be beyond what my poor mind would register.

I shook my head, lining his member to my entrance, "who's the good girl?" he cooed in my ear, and I shuddered, feeling my toes curl in the disgusting pleasure that filled me at hearing him say that. As long as I was a good girl, he was happy, and that's what I want. I want him to be happy so that he doesn't hurt me.

"I...I am," I let out in a hollow whisper, fighting back the scream that wanted to escape me at the feel of his member slowly sliding into my worn walls. "I-I'm the good girl." I panted out as he kissed my lips, swallowing the screams that followed as if wanting to consume them as he consumed me.

Chapter 12

My body felt like it had been hit by a train, and to be honest, it was. I mean, not a train train, but a train. Schalk had fucked me all through the night, and no matter how much I cried, begged, and screamed– he kept going. I knew then, that I had to get out of here, not only was he a psycho but he had to have been a sex addict. I couldn't walk, even if I wanted to. So I was subjected to being wheeled around in a wheelchair by the devil himself.

He pushed me around the beautiful farm house style home that gave off a homey feel more than anything. It felt like at any moment, you'd see kids running around the corner with a ball and cricket bat, talking animatedly about their day at school or how they wanted to go and play outside. It felt like a home, a rich person's home. The beautiful almost brown ceramic tiles, the white walls, the furniture that was both comfort and aesthetically pleasing, and the family pictures on the wall.

They could've fooled me.

I sat in the chair, silent as Schalk pushed me into the family kitchen area where he said his family was having breakfast. I didn't want to be around any of them at this moment, especially his father. Mr Bertus du Toit was one sick fuck, I had no qualms that he was the one who turned his son this way. He created this monster.

Schalk had no problem carrying me around. I had to beg him not to carry me and instead let me sleep in, but he came up with the solution of a wheelchair. How embarrassing. But at this point, I didn't care. I just wanted out of this place.

As we entered the kitchen, an older lady with dirty blonde hair that was pulled into a low messy bun, turned and immediately saw us. Her smile turned wide and happy as her eyes set on Schalk, "my kind!" (my child) she greeted as she ran towards us, engulfing Schalk in a hearty hug. She danced on her feet, her face only reaching his chest as she pulled away from the hug and squeezed his cheeks. "And this must be the future wife?" she had said, gesturing towards me but looking at Schalk and he nodded. "Morning, my name's Rosita," she introduced, luckily I knew the basics of the language so I gave a pursed smile, one that was just purely awkward.

I looked over the woman who was now obviously his mother. Rosita had aged lines, indicating her age which had to have been somewhere in either her 50's or 60's, I'm not sure, but goodness she wasn't aging well, in my opinion. She looked like she could 69, 57, or 43. Her dirty blonde hair was mid length, her eyes were a brown and she gave the appearance of a plain Jane. She was wearing a pair of matching pyjama shorts and a thin strap camisole, showing the freckles that covered her entire body.

Again, maybe she didn't look as glamorous since it was just breakfast.

I can't imagine what mess I probably looked like. Schalk had done my hair and put it in a bun– the rebellious curls making it messy. I was wearing one of his sweatpants and a shirt of his that reached till my knees. I wanted to cover up as much as possible, feeling as violated as one could after the assault that I've been through. No matter how hard I tried to cover up, my neck was still exposed and the dark hickies were out for all of them to see.

She and Schalk continued to chat as we walked over to the circular breakfast table where Mr Bertus was already seated, and Mr du Toit, the COO, that I'd seen only once around the office, and everyone seemed to respect and not treat like the plague, like they treated Schalk. The two men were talking and laughing, and when I was wheeled to the table, they both looked at me for a brief moment and then back at each other, resuming conversation.

I sat, silent, watching Schalk put together a plate for me. He placed three pancakes on my plate and drizzled them in syrup, and then poured me freshly squeezed lemonade that his mother had bragged was the best in the country. I was silent, eating my food and concentrating on my plate alone and not the people here who no doubt knew of my circumstances and didn't care. If I had a phone, I was going to record it all and expose them on social media. The du Toit's were a well-known family and no doubt, the exposure would reveal some things that I'm sure are far beyond my own situation.

How can people be so sick and twisted? I thought to myself as I ate my food.

"So, Ivy, how old are you?" Rosita asked me, taking a bite of her crunchy toast that she seemed to purposely burn and then scrape of the dark parts.

I swallowed the food in my mouth, my eyes immediately going to Schalk to see if I should answer her. His dark eyes were on his own plate which was waffles with ice cream, "22," I answered timidly, my voice coming scratchy and tired. I had lost my voice sometime last night between round 8 and 11, I'm not too sure. I blacked out.

She nodded her head, a smile on her face, "that's a good age," she hummed in approval as she took another bite of her toast, chewing it, and I went back to focus on my own plate, hating how the attention had been on me. "You know, I had my Johannes when I was 20 years old, fell pregnant 19, gave birth in July of the following year, just a day after my birthday. I had my Schalk four years later, when I was 24. It's always best to have children in your twenties, in my opinion," she spoke, taking a sip of her lemonade through a straw, as her eyes watched mine.

My own eyes widened a bit at her words. I cleared my throat, "w-well..." I tried to think of something to say but I was afraid that if I said the wrong thing then Schalk would get upset with me. Right now, I hadn't done anything to upset him.

His mother continued, "Would you like to have children?" she asked me, then laughed lightly, shaking her head, "of course you do. Who doesn't want to have children?" she asked the rhetorical question, looking to her husband, Johannes and Schalk. There was an edge to her words as though to warn me of saying no.

I had always wanted little babies, but of course not when I was 22 years old with some deranged rich man. I had dreamt of going to university, getting a degree, getting a good job and getting on my own two feet, having my own place, own car, own money, and then a man would come into my life. He'd be the perfect man that I could build a life with, I'd fall in love with him, and he'd fall in love with me, and our love would grow stronger with time. We'd probably date for a year or two, then get married, have a traditional wedding and a white wedding, then stay without kids for 2 or 3 years, and then afterwards have 2 children, probably with a four year age gap, and call it a fulfilling life. That, had always been the goal.

However hearing Rosita now talk about children, it caused a chill to run up my spine, at where her mind was and where it would bring Schalk. God...did Schalk want children? Oh Lord, no... No, no, no. I felt my breath begin to come out quick, short and panicked as I looked at her, and the room around us began to spin. I blinked my eyes, and then looked down at my lap, closing my eyes and trying to zone out of whatever this conversation was.

"I would've had more children if it wasn't for my continuous struggle with endometriosis and complications surrounding my womb. I had to have my womb removed before I could even have a little baby girl of my own..." her voice drifted off as if in pain, and I lifted my head to see Mr Bertus had wrapped his arm around her and brought her closer to him, placing a kiss to her lips.

"It's alright, my love. Schalk will give you as many grand-children as possible." He spoke to her and I looked between them, wondering what they were talking about, "all the little boys and the little girls that you can ever ask for."

She seemed to smile at that, "I know my baby won't let me down," she smiled at Schalk who nodded at her. He took my hand in his and brought it to his lips, reaching for the fork on my plate and feeding me. "Sometimes I just get a little sad that I wasn't able to have my own baby girl, you know?" she now spoke to her husband, her foreign words meeting my ears.

She cleared her throat and wiped her tears, "sorry about that. I just get emotional about it sometimes. I always wanted a big family, lots of babies running around, but life," she said with a shrug, her voice back to being normal. "But now things are looking up since you're with my Schalk," she said with a smile, looking at me with a smile that didn't quite reach her eyes, a darkness to her brown eyes that caused the hairs on the back of my neck to rise. "Aren't you happy?" she asked me, her voice one with an edge to it. The kind of edge that said 'you better be'. She sounded so possessive of her son, I wondered if that's where Schalk got it from. He always called me his Ivy, did he get it from her? Owning people. Goodness, what was wrong with this family?

I swallowed, afraid, since I couldn't break away from her eyes. They weren't intense, but I was trying to decipher what the hell was wrong with her. She didn't have the darkness that Mr Bertus did, maybe she was just being as boy mums are. We all know how problematic those can be. "y-yes," I answered, letting her hear exactly what she wanted to hear.

She smiled a genuine smile, "good. You better take care of my Schalk," she looked to him, her eyes pouring with love, "he's my baby," she caressed the side of his face and he moved away from her touch, complaining about her affection as you would see every other child do with the undivided attention from their parents. "You better not break his heart," she added, her eyes breaking from his and back on mine, glaring at me.

What the hell?

My mouth felt dry, "I won't." I found myself croaking out and she nodded her head.

She was silent, finishing up the remainder of her toast and Schalk continued to feed me until my plate was clear. I didn't have an appetite, since I was too busy thinking about how I was going to escape. I just needed a moment and a clear exit. Maybe even a gun and knife because it seems like my escape won't be an easy one, but I sat and thought about how terrible now would be. I couldn't walk and I couldn't scream for help. So I had to just sit there, even though there were knives on the table and the door to the kitchen led directly outside. The fresh air was coming in and if I wanted to run, I could have.

"Did you call Karen?" his father spoke up, breaking the silence around the table. He hadn't looked up from his plate. He continued to enjoy his scrambled eggs and brown bread, a cup of espresso next to his plate, and I part wondered who he was talking to.

Schalk was the one who replied, "I did. I told her to list my penthouse, and get me some homes that we could view later on today or tomorrow. Johannes, I made the decision to stay here. I think when Ivy has the baby, she's going to want her grandmother around, and I don't want to take that away from her."

"Which area are you looking at?" Johannes was the one who spoke up, the men were all looking at each other now. I sat there, fiddling with my own fingers, thinking of what was going to happen to me today. I tried to push the thoughts of Benny aside, not wanting to throw up for the seventh time, since Schalk warned me that if I were to throw up one more time because of Benny, he was going to make me scoop it up and eat it. He told me no man deserved a reaction out of me, not tears, not smiles, nothing. I had to feel nothing. The stench of his body clung to my nose hairs and I tried hard to fight it. I shut my eyes and tried to count to distract myself from the stench.

"Houghton," Schalk played with my hair, his fingers in it, and I winced because my scalp was sensitive for multiple reasons. One, it was a headache that hadn't gone away since I opened my eyes yesterday after the whole cutting my ear off, the other reason was the fact that I fell down the stairs yesterday, and the third reason was that Schalk had been using my hair as some kind rein when he was fucking my pussy like it was the last time he'd get the chance; which I was praying for. "I looked into Sandhurst, but the houses there are beyond my budget. The only two homes on the market there are a R50 million estate, and a R150 million estate."

"Well, what's your budget?" Rosita was piping in now, but I didn't care what they were talking about, all I was doing was praying.

"R20 million." He paused, and I felt his eyes on my face. I opened my eyes to look at him and smile, not wanting him to see me drifting off. I needed to give him my full attention so that he'd remain happy, he continued, "I'm thinking of getting a second home in Camp's Bay, an apartment or something for R10 million so that we can travel easily between Cape Town and Jo'burg."

Jehovah, please get me out of this place. Please, get me away from these people. Please, let me be able to run as far away from them as possible.

"That's good, that's good. I guess I'll call Karen too then, list my house and start looking in Cape Town– " Johannes was speaking and I used that as an opportunity to lean closer to Schalk.

"I need the bathroom," I whispered into his ear, and he nodded his head. He stood from his seat and continued to speak to his family, probably informing them that he was taking me to the loo. I watched as he leaned in and hugged his mother, and walked to his father and brother, and they continued to speak. His mother stood and walked towards me.

She leaned down and wrapped her arms around me in a hug. She pressed her lips to my ear, "listen here, you little poor black girl," her whispering voice met my left, un-harmed ear and I felt my back straighten as an iron rod at the shocking words that just left her lips, "let me tell you a little something about Rosita du Toit, she does anything and everything possible to make sure that her little boys are as happy as can be. If you ever dare to go against me, against my son, and against my family, I'll wring your neck with my own bare hands. Schalk is very special to me, Ivy, and he's got plans for you, and I do too. I give my children whatever they want, and Schalk wants you. I see that look in your eyes, Ivy, no matter how much you try to run, or how far you go, I'll crawl to the edges of this round earth just to find you and bring your black ass back to my son." She pulled away and straightened up, looking right into my eyes with a deranged glint that belonged to a mad woman.

She then smiled, her eyes becoming warm, "do visit again, my daughter. Can I call you that? Can I call you my daughter?" she asked, her tone becoming cheery. "I mean, it shouldn't be a problem," she shrugged, "we're going to be family."

Chapter 13

I stood, looking out the floor to ceiling, wall to wall, windows overlooking downtown Sandton in Schalk's penthouse. I wrapped my arms around my midsection, Schalk's cologne mixed with the scent of Marlboro that clung onto his hoodie that I was wearing, met my nostrils. I found myself leaning in and breathing in the scent, slowly having become addicted to it. I didn't think I'd ever like the smell of men's cologne mixed with cigarettes, yet here I was, breathing it in almost like stealing the breath of a flower.

The sun was just rising and I was watching the light orange-ish tint in the sky. You could see the faintest of the half-moon hidden behind a skyscraper. I watched it with a small smile, hearing the background noise of the news in the background talking about the current economic decline. I had the distant thought of how this country was in shambles as I stood there, socks on my feet since the marble floors felt too cold for my sensitive feet. My curly hair was a rest's nest, but I didn't care. I had showered some time ago, and Schalk was moving around the penthouse, gathering certain items and packing them. He preferred to do it himself, he told me, he liked packing what he felt was important and leaving the rest behind.

We'd been house hunting the day before and I still couldn't wrap my head around it. I couldn't believe that I had actually been house hunting, first of all. It seemed whatever deluded thought that ran through Schalk's mind was more serious than I thought that it had been. I'd thought it was a case of him having a crush on a black girl or something sick like that, a fetish or something, not anything serious. But when he'd gotten me up early yesterday, dressed me in a Jean Paul Gaultier dress and YSL black heels, and driven me to view homes that I didn't even know existed in my country. The houses we'd looked at were far beyond what my imagination had thought possible for little town girl me with dreams of a modest life.

I, in no means, aspired for a big life. I always wanted a modest life, a life with a four bedroom beautiful home, a two car garage, private school for my kids, a great job where I had enough holidays and free time to hang out with my children, and being able to just be happy. That had always been my dream, but I was watching as things seemed to be moving hundreds of kilometres around me and I didn't know how to slow it down.

I heard Schalk set another box down in the living room behind me, and I found myself turning around now. The brown box was open and several things stuck out, too large to be contained in the box. "What's that?" I asked him, pointing towards it.

He looked at it briefly, "a canvas." He answered.

"Like, for painting?" no, for cooking. Of course for painting! My mind replied to me sarcastically. So I thought to move on quickly from the silly question, "you paint?" I decided to add, raising an eyebrow.

He looked at it, and then at me, shrugging his shoulders. My eyes moved all over his naked torso, taking in the sight of his abs and strong chest. He had tattoos around his biceps, and all over his back. He looked like a God before me, his body that of perfection. He wore a pair of sweatpants that hung low on his hips, showing off his v line, and I cleared my throat and looked away. When I looked into his eyes, he was smirking, obviously in silence because of my ogling, "actually, no. I don't paint, I sketch. I'm an engineer, sketching is what I do best. I had a canvas," he looked back at it almost as if he didn't know why he had, "just because." He finished off.

I hummed, nodding my head. "I've never painted before," I found myself saying, looking at the canvas and covering the distance between Schalk and I. I reached the box, reaching for the canvas and taking it into my own hands. "I went to a public school, and the only time we painted was when we were in primary school, on plain white pages. The paint was cheap, and I remember it seeping through the pages because it was more water than paint..." I trailed off at the memory of it. "That was...only once," I revealed to him, looking over the canvas and touching it because it was the first time I was seeing one.

I saw them paint in movies and shows, but never did it myself. What did I look like heading to a shop and buying a canvas when we needed rice, or bread, or food? Painting was never something that I thought I could do.

Schalk came over to the box, opening it even further and pressing the top of it to the sides as he reached inside it. He pulled out several paint containers and held them in his arms, "well, there's no time like the present." He said as he pulled out a set of brand new paintbrushes still in their packaging.

"Oh, I don't think I can paint that well," I attempted to argue but he wasn't having any of it.

"Of course you can," he answered me, walking over to the dining table and setting the paint down on the expensive looking table.

I shook my head, but walked to the table as well, "oh please, what if I just ruin the canvas or something?"

"Then I'll get another one." He let out a chuckle, placing the paint on the expensive glass table, "it's just a canvas, Ivy." He said lightly, soothing my concerns. I don't know why that hit me harder than it did, it's just a canvas, Ivy. I came from a life where things weren't 'just this' or 'just that'. It took a lot to get it, especially surviving off my grandma's pension. It wasn't easy, so everything that we owned meant that we had to treasure it and not waste it. So I always feared ruined things, or wasting things, because I knew how much went into getting it in the first place.

"...yeah..." I said lowly, setting it on the table and watching as he tore the packaging, pulling out the paint brushes and setting them neatly along the table. "It's...it's just a canvas." I repeated, my words feeling heavy and unsure. I picked up one of the paint brushes and looked down at the paint containers that he'd already popped open for me, "what if I...you know? I don't know, what if it's horrible though?"

He stood, "not possible. Anything you do is always perfect to me. You could paint a black dot, and I'd build a museum and display it," he answered, leaning in and placing a peck to my forehead, and walked away, leaving me with his words. Wow.

He returned with a sheet of paper and several pencils and pens, sitting across from me at the table. "I'll sketch, while you paint," he told me, but my eyes were on the canvas as I dipped the paintbrush in paint and began stroking against the white of it, covering it in paint, without a clear plan in mind.

Schalk sat across from me, the sound of pencil against paper on a glass table met my ears as we sat in silence for a few. I then decided to speak up, feeling like the silence was getting to me too much. I hated silence, I came from a noisy home and as a result hated it when it was too quiet, because I found it eerie. "This is so soothing," I said happily, unable to keep the genuine smile off my face as I dipped the brush in another colour, bringing it to the canvas. "I see why people do this all the time. It's fun," I looked up from my painting and met Schalk's dark blue eyes already on mine. My genuine smile slightly wavered at the way that he watched me. His stare was always so intense.

"Are you...are you always this...this intense?" I asked him, breaking our eye contact and looking down at my canvas.

He was silent for a bit and I heard the sound of pencil on paper again, and he resumed his sketching, "I don't know how to answer that." He told me.

"Do you ever, I don't know, do you ever just laugh? Like genuinely, deep from the pits of your stomach kind of laugh," I described, wondering the mystery of the man who sat across from me– the deranged man who was keeping me locked away in his castle from the rest of the world. He didn't seem all that human to me, even when I touched him, his skin, his body, everything, it felt otherworldly. It was so strange. Maybe my mind was creating a different version of the man before me because of what he had put me through, I don't know.

"Of course I do," he chuckled, "I'm human." It sure doesn't feel like it. The words died in my mind, knowing that daring to utter them would be me possibly signing my death wish.

"You know, I have this thing where I snort when I laugh really hard. It's so gross," I commented with a head shake, laughing lightly. "My mother hates it when that happens, my father thinks it's just a bit weird. My grandmother thinks it's normal, since she's the most used to it. I spent most of my time with her, and I'm the most comfortable around her, obviously." I paused, mid stroke, feeling my mind run with what I said. I bit my bottom lip, silent for a bit, "my mother hates a lot of things." Sometimes I think she might hate me, are the words I wish to say, but opt not to because saying them out loud might make them true.

My relationship with my mother was strained and she was like a stranger to me. To be fair, my relationship between my father and I was also strained, but when he saw me, I saw him as my father; a friend, a protector, a cool dude, I don't know. Maybe that's just my mummy issues trying to create something more of the absent man. I don't know what I'd do if both of my parents couldn't stand me.

I let out a deep breath, puffing out my cheeks as I picked up a different brush and dipped it in paint, "there was this one time when I was visiting my uncle for the December holidays when I was in grade 10. My uncle and my aunt, his wife, had decided that they wanted to paint their house a new colour. So, I went with my uncle to the store to pick out the paint. She had wanted to paint their home this sapphire blue kind of paint, and one thing about my uncle, he's a cheap man. He likes to save wherever he can. So when we got to the store, he got the cheapest brand of paint that had this really weird name," I began to giggle, "and I told him, 'I don't think you should go for a brand that just came out, like, a month ago'. And he was, like, 'shut up this is adult stuff, mind your own business' and I let him pick it. I thought 'you know what, he's right, I don't know anything when it comes to paint'. We get home with the buckets of paint, and since he and I are close and I really wanted to help him paint the house, since he didn't want to hire anyone because they were too expensive and he'd rather spend the next week painting the house, I decided to lend a helping hand." At this point, I couldn't stop laugh.

"He opened the first bucket of paint, and it was this purple-ish colour, like a dark blue but so dark it was purple. I laughed so hard, I think the mountains there still echo my laugh," at this point my grin was huge and my laugh was almost uncontrollable. "And he still tried to play it off, and he was like 'yeah, well, the paint just has to marinate a bit', and that made me laugh even harder because I knew my aunt was going to kill him once she saw that colour. So, he got to painting, and painting, the whole day, until he had painted one side of the house before it was too late and we went inside. Later on that night, it began to rain," I continued the tale, still laughing but getting close to what I wanted to say. "Then morning came and I was the first one up. I ran outside to check on the paint because I thought the rain was going to wipe it off, or something like that. And when I got there, the paint wasn't purple anymore but a sort of blue that wasn't sapphire blue...but a dark blue..." I paused, looking up to meet Schalk's eyes that were on mine already, his hand moving quickly over the paper, "like yours. So every time that I look into your eyes, I remember the December holiday dark blue house where I spent one of my best Christmases," I finished with a smile and shrug, going back to painting.

It sucked that those dark blue eyes that brought nothing but pain to me, reminded me of some of my best years. I seemed to think about it a lot too because I couldn't imagine looking into them and thinking of the horrors that he had put me through, it would drive me insane.

"Okay...I think I'm done," I said, looking down at the canvas with a smile. "It's abstract though," I tried to explain with a nervous smile as I picked it up and looked at it sideways and then looked at Schalk, "you ready?"

He nodded his head and then I bit my lip, "no, no, wait, show me yours first. I'm nervous to show you mine," I said, feeling my heart race with nerves at what he'd think of my painting.

He set his pencil down and then lifted the sheet in my direction, allowing me to set my eyes on a perfect sketch of my face. My jaw dropped at the shaded lines and sketch of me smiling, my eyes downcast, and my features gentle and perfect. He had captured me all the way to the rebellious hairs on my eyebrows and the pimple on the left side of my forehead. It was picture perfect and I looked at it, unable to say anything for a moment. "Oh...my God," I let out in an awed whisper, reaching a hand out to trace the sketch as if it would come to life and I'd be stroking my own features. "You're amazing. I mean, your drawing is amazing." I looked down nervously at my own, "I don't think I should show you mine."

"Nonsense. Show me," Schalk encouraged as he slide the sheet to the side and I sighed.

"Promise me that you won't laugh," I looked at him seriously and he smirked, nodding his head.

"I promise."

"Okay..." I cleared my throat and then lifted the canvas, turning it in his direction. Schalk was silent, his eyes widening a bit, his brows raised, and his face one of shock as he looked at my canvas. Before I noticed the twitch of his lips, and not even a second letter, the loudest laugh erupted from his lips. He threw his head back and I sat there abashed at his reaction, "you promised you wouldn't laugh!" I exclaimed, as he laughed so hard, I was stuck between throwing the canvas at him or being in shock that he was laughing because of me. "It's a cat!" I tried to argue.

"With 8 legs?" he countered, still laughing uncontrollably, seeming as though he was moments from tears.

"That's the fur!" I shouted back, explaining to him, and he laughed even harder, falling off his chair.

"It has 8 hairs?!" I couldn't help but laugh with him, finding his laugh to be contagious as we both struggled to calm down. In that moment it felt like I wasn't sitting and laughing with a man whose bruises still marred my body, in that moment it felt a lot like I was sitting with somebody that I loved and trusted, the space between us one of safety, comfort and joy. I realised then, watching him laugh and struggling to breathe from my own laughter, that if I could stay in that moment for some time, a longer time than I was in it, I'd be perfectly content.

Chapter 14

"**Y**ou ever going to look away?" I heard the voice that belonged to one of my close cousins, Heinrich. I felt his hand on my shoulder, and I shook my head, my eyes on the honey beauty that was dancing in the middle of the penthouse with a few of my other family members' girlfriends. My Ivy was dressed in a cherry red mesh mini dress with long sleeves, her hair was free and perfectly done courtesy of the celebrity hair stylist I had called in a few hours ago. She looked so perfect with the lights shining off her skin and the smile on her face as she and Heinrich's girlfriend of four years danced to whatever pop song they'd just put on.

The two women seemed to have taken a good liking to each other. "She's perfection..." I mused, my voice coming out as thinly veiled adoration for the woman that I was going to spend the rest of my life with. Her skin glowed with a certain essence that let me know that she was already pregnant, she just didn't know it yet. "When did you get back?" I hadn't turned my head away from looking at my woman, watching her dance was more than enough for me. I had half the mind to walk over to her and rip that dress that barely covered anything off– the way that the red thong she wore underneath was slightly visible, the peak of her nipples against the material, the way the off-the-shoulder dress accented her collarbones and bone structure, and the perfect curves of her hourglass petite figure. Oh, how'd I ever get so lucky?

Heinrich was one of the top lawyers in the country, defending the kind of men who had pockets that ran so deep, there wasn't an end to it. He had the best law firm in the country, and the whole of the southern, eastern, and western Africa. He was a busy man, and we didn't get to see each other a lot because he always travelled due to work. He represented the president of the country and the several elite families that ran a mafia that Heinrich managed to keep hidden.

"Just an hour ago," he responded, "I didn't want to miss the opportunity of seeing the very woman who has my baby cousin Schalk on his knees," he chuckled, and I turned my head to face him, a grin on my face as I brought the Corona beer bottle to my lips, drinking from it.

"Aren't you only 6 years older than me?" I countered, "I'm not a baby." Heinrich enjoyed being annoying from time to time when it came to me. I was one of the few who managed to see his more light hearted side, and he was one of the few who managed to see my more laid back side. Other than that, Heinrich was more of a du Toit than I was, he was sicker than me, and that's a lot because even Ruan fears the man.

This man's a legend, Ruan spoke up, interrupting my throats. Don't get too close to him, Schalk! Just...take a step back, please...for fucks sakes, take a step back! I found myself taking a step back because I didn't want the headache that came with Ruan yelling at me.

"Hey, I was changing your nappies when you were this big," he made a small notion with his hands, the size of probably the smallest baby bird you've ever seen, "do you remember when you peed on me?" he reminded me, a smirk on his face, his Burberry suit not at all like the people in the room who were dressed in more casual wear since this was a braai (barbecue/barbeque).

Oh God, we were only 6 months old! Ruan argued exasperatedly, tired of hearing the same thing from Heinrich.

He can never let us live that down... Botha added in the same tone, as if rolling his eyes.

Sakkie let out a chuckle, I don't know, I find it kind of endearing.

I know I say this often, but Sakkie? Ruan called.

Yes? Sakkie replied.

I really....really...from the pits of my stomach, the deepest corners of my heart, from the very essence of my soul...I really, really....like, as really as it can get, hate you. There are absolutely no words to say this but fuck, I loathe you. Like, deeply, thoroughly– Ruan went on.

Sakkie cleared his throat, I heard you...-

Like unequivocally, limitlessly, wholeheartedly, full-mindedly, richly–

I said I fucking get it!

–hate you…

"I was only six months old, dumb ass. I should piss on you again," I told him, turning my attention to the braai stand that we had set up on the balcony since I didn't want to be too far away from my woman.

"Where's Johannes?" Heinrich asked me, accepting a drink from one of our servers. Heinrich was a lot like Johannes, they wore suits, were faces and heads of successful companies, and they were both gentlemen. Heinrich never drove, I don't think he's ever been behind the wheel in his life since he's always being driven. He doesn't open doors, doesn't lift a hand unless it's to accept what he's being handed. He drinks whisky and smokes his father's old pipe.

"He's gone out with his other friends," I said with a scoff, "his normal friends," I added, shivering in distaste at the word normal. Johannes liked to exclude himself from the rest of the family, he saw himself as better, always putting distance between us like we were the plague. He thought that if he wasn't around us, then he wouldn't be too much like us. Yet he always has toys.

"Oh, well, if it isn't Nicolaas," Heinrich spoke up and I looked up from the steak that I was braai-ing and turned my head to look at the young man who was striding towards us.

I let out a dry chuckle, "when was the last time we saw you?" I asked him rhetorically because it had been over a year. Nicolaas was like Johannes, they wanted no parts of being du Toit's, but unlike Johannes who still had a very sick and twisted side, Nicolaas had taken after his French mother. He and his mother were as close as mother and son could get. Nicolaas didn't even see himself as a du Toit, he disassociated himself from the name and from us, and he poorly concealed his distaste towards us. Nicolaas' father was Heinrich's older brother, Frederich. Frederich and Heinrich had a 10 year age gap, and Frederich had followed more of a family role while Heinrich preferred living the life of a bachelor. It seemed the toy that he had now was an Arab beauty by the name of Aadilah. Aadilah's been with Heinrich for four years, and something tells me when relationships hit that mark, they turn into a marriage.

"I think it was on Heinrich's birthday," Nicolaas didn't call Heinrich 'uncle' since Heinrich hated it, and preferred his name. Uncle was too 'friendly' he'd said.

Nicolaas walked over to the railing, leaning against it, his body towering over both Heinrich and I. Nicolaas was a 6'6 hockey playing, French wine loving boy who had on more than one occasion told us what sick and demented individuals we were.

"Hm," I hummed, going back to braai-ing the meat, "I don't know how long you can keep acting like you're a Le Roux, when you're a du Toit," I told him, looking over into his blue eyes. He didn't back down from my stare, he held it, and I could see the way that his eyes were blank that as much as he tried to fight it, it would only be a matter of time before he was just like me, just like Heinrich, and just like the rest of the du Toit's. "You're not French, you're Afrikaans, like us, Nicolaas. I can't wait for the day that you realise it," I said, looking down at the meat and placing it on trays as I added some more onto the braai stand.

I set the tongs down and got to taking the first piece of boerewors, "I don't remember the last time I had a lekker braai," (good/delicious) Heinrich stated, walking over towards me and grabbing his own piece, both of us standing by the smoke, coughing occasionally from the thick smoke.

"How's school?" Heinrich asked his nephew and he shrugged, his eyes looking side wards at the view of the city instead of us. Heinrich wanted Nicolaas to follow in his footsteps. He told me that he saw potential in Nicolaas to be an excellent attorney. "Well, you know that I want you to work under me. I know you can be a good lawyer and I need another du Toit by my side. I can't trust Schalk, he'd have blown up my building by now, and Johannes is into engineering and running his father's company."

Nicolaas chuckled, nodding his head at the comment of my hot-headed attitude, "sure," he said simply, shrugging, "I don't mind."

I looked to the side, looking into the penthouse, feeling like I hadn't looked at my woman in forever. She was still dancing, except now, Aadilah was teaching her how to belly dance, since Aadilah was a belly dancer. I watched the way that my Ivy's body moved as she mimicked Aadilah's dancing, and Ivy felt my stare on her because she looked up, meeting my eyes. I watched as her eyes widened and then she hurriedly turned around and faced Aadilah again. I chuckled, tuning back into the conversation between nephew and uncle.

"Yeah, grade 11 is next year." Nicolaas nodded at whatever Heinrich had been saying, probably lecturing him about how important his marks were. "So, when's the wedding?"

Nicolaas turned his attention to me, obviously steering the conversation away from him.

"7 weeks from now," I revealed, attending to the meat. "We've already met with her family, and everything's been sorted. Her father wanted 15 cows for her," I scoffed, shaking my head. Buying fifteen cows wasn't an issue for me, it was how I had sat across from the man and he had bragged about raising his daughter so well, and taking care of her, and now needing me to prove myself. He didn't know that I was aware that he was a deadbeat father, but of course, since he was her father and due to my Ivy's beliefs, I wasn't going to kill him until after the wedding. "And an extra R80, 000 in hand. In hindsight, he probably saw the cars we came with and knew that he could get any amount out of us. So, since meeting her father and uncles has gone smoothly, preparations are fully under way," I revealed to them.

"Free up your schedules," I continued, picking up my beer, "you're going to be my groomsmen." Nicolaas chuckled and Heinrich congratulated me. "So, let's have a toast," I gestured and Heinrich lifted his glass of whisky and Nicolaas lifted his glass of French wine, "to being a du Toit," I said with a smirk, my eyes meeting Nicolaas' blue eyes.

You're a du Toit, kid. It's only a matter of time... Botha spoke, and it was as if Nicolaas had heard him as he broke our eye contact and mumbled a 'cheers'.

Chapter 15

I bit my lip, slowly walking through the aisles in the store, picking up whatever snacks I wanted to have. I looked behind me, immediately connecting with dark blue eyes that were watching me. Schalk was leaning against his Bentley, sitting on the hood with a cigarette between his lips, his eyes hooded and watching me like they always did. His stare was so intense, it made me feel hot. I could tell what he was thinking– could see the hunger behind those orbs for me.

He was dressed in a pair of black jeans and a black graphic tee, the shades that he had been wearing were on my face because I thought they were cool and wanted to wear them myself. The petrol attendant was filling up the tank, the Engen garage had two other cars, and some of the petrol attendants were taking pictures of the car. He didn't pay attention to any of that because his eyes were glued to me, and even though my eyes were covered by the shades that I'd stolen off his face, it felt like he could see right through them.

I turned my back to him, grabbing a bunch of sweets, and Mexican Chili Simba chips, a Redbull, and a coke before I headed over to the counter. I caught my reflection in the camera by the door, showing me my figure dressed in a black leather pair of pants that hugged my figure and a black long sleeve crop top that ended right underneath my breasts, showing off my body from my ribs down to belly button.

I smiled at the lady behind the counter as she rang up my items, "R185," she told me and I scoffed at the price. This country was absolutely crazy.

I handed her the crisp R200 note and took the items, walking back outside, hearing G-Eazy and Halsey's Him & I that was playing from the car as I approached Schalk. As soon as I approached him, he got off the hood of the car and met me halfway, wrapping his arm around me and pulling me into his body before he placed his lips on mine, kissing me like it was just the two of us.

I'd gotten too comfortable in the three weeks that I've been with Schalk, falling into the world that Schalk had introduced me to. Life felt like a movie; as long as I stayed on his good side. He took me shopping in Spain, and we went paragliding in Switzerland, I rode camels in Egypt and partied with Idris Elba in New York City. I was living a life that had me forgetting that I wasn't here by free will. I wore my own Rolex watch on one wrist, Cartier bracelets on the other, a diamond necklace worth R200, 000 around my neck, limited edition Jimmy Choo on my feet that I got as a gift from the Managing Director of the company. I mean, who could say that? That they got

Jimmy Choo's as a gift from the MD himself? Me. I could say that.

The night air in Sandton had suddenly become too chilly. I could taste his cigarette on my tongue, his cologne filled my nostrils, and his hands were warm on my waist, bringing me so close as if I was going to disappear at any moment. I was experiencing pure bliss at the moment, and I couldn't even imagine leaving his side. I was in heaven, enjoying helicopter rides to dinner dates and seeing a side of Schalk I never knew existed.

He finally allowed me to breathe and I took in a long breath, my eyes clouded with tears from how long he had been kissing me as if he was doing it with the intention of sucking my soul out of me. "I got you a Redbull," I told him, looking up at him, my eyes clashing with dark blue ones that gazed at me with a darkness that I'd become too comfortable with. I looked away and stepped out of his arms, taking his hand in my other one as we walked back to the car. He opened the driver's side, sliding in, pulling me in with him and settling me in his lap.

He pressed his face to the side of my face, breathing me in, and his nose brushed the tip of my left ear. He breathed me in like he couldn't get enough of my scent. He brought his hand around my neck, wrapping it and tightening his grip before he placed open mouthed kisses all over my jaw. I closed my eyes, sighing in pleasure at his ministrations and feeling my toes curl in pleasure. He brought his lips closer to mine, then placed several sweet pecks on my lips, his eyes open, peering into mine with an intensity that felt as orgasmic as his strokes during sex.

"Stop," I whispered out weakly, hearing the unsteadiness of my voice, the drunken desire, the fear, and the excitement. "Stop looking at me like that," I continued, my eyes searching for any bit of hesitance. He looked at me like he felt everything fully, like whatever he was feeling for me was beyond words, as if he was experiencing it with every fibre of his being.

Have you ever looked at someone and knew that you were everything to them?

There's a sense of fear that comes with it, the way they look at you, the power that you know you hold. There's nothing like looking into someone's eyes and seeing that you are everything to them.

It's funny because it's what I've always wanted, but not like this.

He didn't say anything only pulled away from me and began driving the car with me in his lap. I rested my back to the door, my eyes on his face my left hand reaching into his hair, playing with the hair at the back of his head. Schalk felt like a teenage dream– a model-like, wealthy man who smokes cigarettes, has tattoos, abs that you could grate on and the aura of a bad boy. There was nothing like it, nothing like him.

The music was blasting, the top of the car was down, the smooth white leather seats of his Bentley had become our home, the night lights of the best city in Africa surrounding us like rebellious stars, skyscrapers made of glass that reflected the very essence of a city that brought dreams to life. There was nothing like Sandton, nothing like the luxury cars that were racing in the now night hours of a Saturday night, cars blasting music, buildings that belonged to giant companies, planes flying above, a dark sky, partygoers walking along the streets of every open bar, club and restaurant. There was nothing like Sandton.

Schalk finally pulled the car into a parallel parking spot with ease. I looked at the building before me, "Boneshakers Body Art," I said aloud, looking at the tattoo shop that we were parked in front of. There were people walking up and down the street, ladies in party dresses, men laughing with their friends, drinks in hands, people dancing, others screaming as they walked to wherever they were going. "What are we doing here?" I asked Schalk as he cut the engine and opened the door. He carried me in his arms, getting out of the car with me in his arms and setting me down as we walked around the car, heading into the shop.

He didn't answer me, only held my hand in his as we walked side by side and entered the cool tattoo shop. There was someone sitting at the door, getting a tattoo on his arm, except he looked too young to be getting one. He seemed like he was only 13 or 14 at most. A tattoo artist; a man with dreadlocks, looked up when he saw us enter and then looked away, resuming his tattooing.

The sound of buzzing and needle meeting skin met my ears as Schalk walked us further into the tattoo shop and turned left, the lights suddenly becoming red and feeling like we had walked into a sex dungeon. There were different tattoo art works along the wall, pictures of people who'd gotten body tattoos from the tip of their heads to their very toes. I pushed myself further into Schalk's body until we entered a room and a bald headed woman who was covered in colourful ink from the tip of her head to her toes greeted us. She looked terrifying, but in a cool way. Her face was covered in ink and she was only wearing a pair of panties, her breasts completely tattooed and nipples pierced, "hey," she greeted with a smile as she stood to shake my hand but not Schalk's.

Schalk had dropped my hand and walked over to the bed, taking off his shirt and setting it on the chair right beside the bed. The lady seemed to have been expecting our arrival because she had her tools set on the table next to the bed, "so, how are you feeling?" she asked me as I walked closer to the bed, getting closer to Schalk.

I found it weird that she was asking me since Schalk was the one in the chair, "good," I answered with a smile, hearing the grunge music that was playing in the room. She nodded her head.

"You ready? This your first time?" she asked me, seeming to only be conversing with me. I furrowed my brows, looking to Schalk and then back at her because I knew I had better luck with getting answers from her than him.

"Excuse me? First time doing what, exactly?" I asked her, watching as she held up a tattoo gun and I took a hesitant step back.

"Tattooing someone," she answered with a laugh, noticing my hesitancy. She looked back at Schalk, "you're going to be tattooing him today." She explained.

I looked at Schalk, my eyes widening as I shook my head, "wh-what? Oh no, I can't tattoo, I can't even draw a stick figure. Remember when you laughed at my cat?" I reminded Schalk, wondering why he'd want me to tattoo him when I couldn't draw or paint to save my life.

She didn't care, she handed me the gun, gesturing for me to get closer, "don't worry. It'll be easy," she watched me, beckoning me with her gaze and I slowly got closer to her, taking the gun from her hesitantly, "it's just your name."

"My...my name?" I repeated, my eyes widening some more as I looked at Schalk who now had a new cigarette between his lips, watching me. He nodded his head, gesturing towards his heart, "Right here, my soet Ivy."

"Schalk...oh my God," I gasped as the lady approached me and began adjusting my hold on the gun. She pushed me closer to him, all while telling me what to press to start inking his skin. I tried to argue but she wasn't having any of it.

"I said I want her to do it," he voiced, his tone chilling as he looked at the lady with the tattoos who had been holding my hand to guide mine to tattooing his skin. She let go of my hand as if it were made of fire and apologised profusely, then those dark blue eyes looked at mine, "your name, babygirl." He lifted his left hand and gently caressed my face, brushing his thumb against my lips, "right above my heart," he continued, his fingers dancing against my skin, moving with expertise, "if I could, I would've ripped my heart out of my chest and had you tattoo that, but for now, cover me in your name, babygirl, mark me as you please because

I'm yours…" he lifted his head from the bed and pulled me into a passionate kiss, "only yours."

I bit my lip as he pulled away and took the tattoo gun, pressing as the lady had instructed and met the needle with his skin. My brows furrowed, feeling the intensity of his stare on his face as Avril Lavigne's Bite Me played in the background. My hands were unsteady, unsure and afraid, but I kept moving them, branding him with my name on his skin; marring him.

Chapter 16

Schalk's driver pulled the Bentley Bentayga into the entrance of the all exclusive Vivid Roux Cucina which was a restaurant on the waters of an exclusive private man-made beach in the south of Jo'burg. I didn't know about the place, didn't even know that it existed until an hour ago when Schalk revealed to me that he was taking me to a restaurant that was 'invite-only'.

The door was immediately opened for the both of us, Schalk stepping out on the other side, exiting the car with me. I wrapped the mink fur coat tighter around me, breathing in the night air as I walked around the back of my car, my eyes connecting with dark blue ones.

Schalk looked like he was worth a million dollars tonight. He was dressed in a Dolce & Gabbana sequin-embellished three-piece suit. It was made of a black wool with long sleeves, two front flap pockets, a fitted waistline and slim cut that moulded his body so well, I could barely keep my eyes to myself. He paired the suit with a pair of black leather Valentino Garavani rockstud derby shoes, and a TAG Heuer watch he'd gotten custom made with my blood trapped inside the various diamonds it had adorning it.

He watched me as I walk towards him and pulled me closer to his body as we approached the doors. "Mr du Toit," the man at the door spoke, dressed in a crisp white suit, fresh white towels rested on his arm as he nodded his head respectfully at us. "Mrs du Toit," he addressed me, not once meeting my eyes, "it's a pleasure to have you honour our invite," the man spoke as he gestured with an arm in the direction of where we were meant to go.

My eyes looked around the place. The restaurant was unlike anything I'd ever seen before, from the glass floor that was built under the water, an array of colourful fish swimming under us, the water of the beach and the sound of the waves crashing around us. I was stuck between feeling anxious and nervous about being surrounded by so much water, or being in pure awe at the beauty of the crystal blue water. The restaurant was built in the water, encasing us with views of fish I never knew even existed. Beautiful harp music was being played, the sound seeming to bounce off the glass walls, vibrating the ground under us as Schalk slowly slid my coat off me. The feel of his fingertips on my exposed skin made me feel on fire.

I was dressed in a navy thigh slit floor length gown. The dress was made of lustrous silk navy satin with a high straight neckline in a sleeveless cut. The front of the dress was gathered with a flattering twist at the waist that subtly defined the elegant silhouette and draped fluidly over my curves, finishing with a thigh slit for extra drama and revealing legs. I wore the dress with a navy blue Jimmy Choo heel and my hair was curled and free. It was the only way that I wore it because I didn't want anyone to see my ear.

I sucked in a breath, feeling Schalk close the distance between us, his front to my back. His member pressed between my ass as he ran his nose along my exposed neck, causing heat to erupt all over my skin. He brought his lips to my right ear and I could feel his smile as he saw his ear to mine, he placed a kiss on it and then pulled away from me, allowing me to take a seat at the table. "This place is amazing," I said with a smile as I looked around.

"Good evening," the chef approached our table smiling at Schalk and then briefly glancing at me, keeping his hands behind his back. "I am chef Mulder, and I'm pleased that you're joining us for tonight. The restaurant and myself hold a three star Michelin award, so you're in safe hands," he spoke and then looked at Schalk, "Mr Schalk du Toit, it's lovely seeing you again."

"Of course, Daan. I'm terribly sorry about what happened with Mia," Schalk spoke, not sounding very apologetic at all. I was used to him at this point, he wasn't really an emotional person...or a person at all.

Those seemed to be the words that made Chef Mulder swallow, as if holding back tears as his eyes looked to the floor. "Ye...yeah," he cleared his throat, looking as if he wanted to run as far away as he could from our table.

"Wh..." I know I shouldn't have asked, but I couldn't help it. One man was becoming highly emotional, while the other seemed like he wanted to get started on appetisers, "what happened to Mia?" I found myself asking, not sounding any bit uncouth but my voice low and gentle, holding question towards both men.

"Mia...is...was my daughter. She was in a relationship with Johannes," the chef explained, his eyes still low as if he couldn't bear to look up, "they went on holiday and there was a bit of an accident." He explained heavily, his voice holding nothing but pure pain and anguish, sounding as a parent who was trying to keep it together would.

Schalk continued on from the man, his voice not at all wavering, in fact it seemed even colder, "they were attacked by a puma, and Mia was mauled. It was on the same day that I brought you to my parents' house." I thought back to it, the only time I was at his parents' house was the day that he had killed Benny, cut off my ear and the whole load of it. I remember seeing Johannes at the breakfast table in the morning, he'd been talking to his father, both men laughing and talking about what I could only assume to be mundane things since they were speaking in Afrikaans. Johannes hadn't looked at as if he had been attacked by a puma, he didn't have any scars on him at all.

I looked at Schalk and the way that he watched me, as if he was waiting for me to piece it together. I felt the hairs on the back of my neck stand, goosebumps rise on my skin, my stomach churn and suddenly I realised that Mia hadn't been killed by a puma at all. Johannes had killed her, because they were a sick family. A bunch of sick individuals that I've been stuck with. I watched as a smirk spread across Schalk's face as if to say 'that's it, you got it now' and then he turned and looked back at the chef who hadn't moved from his spot. "You can go on Daan, you look like you're going to cry. This better not affect our food, keep your emotions in check."

I watched as the chef walked away and kept my eyes away from Schalk's dark blue ones, choosing to focus on the bread on the table. I grabbed some of it, breaking it into pieces and praying that I wasn't going to get sick. I'd been feeling under the weather these past couple of days, I threw up anything that I ate. I could barely keep it together if I picked up the smell of eggs, and Schalk loved himself some scrambled eggs.

"Are you feeling okay? Are you feeling nauseous?" Schalk asked me and I looked up to him, meeting his eyes with a tight lipped smile as I shook my head. He seemed to be used to it at this point. I assumed I was getting sick because of all of the travel that I was doing. I was jetlagged, jumping into plane after plane, partying it up, having a good time, constantly on the move. We only got back three days ago and the new house that Schalk had bought for us, mind you, was done with the few renovations that he'd wanted.

I picked up the glass of water and brought it to my lips, "I'm okay. I'm just praying I don't get sick here, again. Oh God, please tell me they're not going to serve fish because I just know I'm going to vomit all over these floors," I said with a new panic as I looked at Schalk with a nervous gaze.

He chuckled, shaking his head no, "I spoke to Daan before we got here. I told him no fish, and nothing that smells too strong. The prettier it looks, the better." Schalk explained before a server appeared out of nowhere.

"Can I interest you in some Ruinart champagne?" the server asked holding up a bottle of champagne and looked at us.

"Ooh," I said with an excited smile, eager to get to drinking just a little bit of alcohol. In all the time that I'd been spending with Schalk, he hadn't let me take a drop of alcohol. Now, I wasn't an alcoholic or someone who went out of their way to drink, but a sip here and a sip there usually occurred, but I hadn't taken a sip here or a sip there in three weeks. "Don't mind i-"

I looked up from holding up my champagne flute to find Schalk glaring into the eyes of the server who looked like he was getting his soul sucked out of him, "she won't be having alcohol. I already said that." Schalk deadpanned and the server nodded his head apologising profusely and running away from the table.

I put the glass down and looked at him with furrowed brows, "erm...okay..." I trailed off, looking at him in question. For a second my mind fought with itself on whether to ask what was wrong or to simply ignore it and pretend like nothing happened, "what was that about?" I finally managed to say, looking back at the spot that the water had been standing at and then back at Schalk. "Why can't I have a sip of that champagne? I hadn't even heard of it before, so I wanted to get a taste," I said as respectfully and delicately as I could, not wanting to get on his bad side. I wanted to remain in the good girl category that I'd been thriving in for weeks, and as long as I was good, life was even better for me.

"Because," he began, sitting back in his chair as another server arrived and started placing our starters on the table, doing so quickly and silently, "it's still early days. I don't want anything bad to happen. Alcohol isn't good for you."

I laughed lightly, shaking my head a bit, "alcohol isn't good for you either. Even smoking," I added, picking up the fork, "actually, especially smoking. You don't see me stopping you from getting that Marlboro smoke pack," I accused light-heartedly, finding it comical that he was telling me what was good for me and what wasn't. I mean, who was he to talk? Of course, I wouldn't dare say that aloud. "What is this?" I asked him, gesturing at what was on my plate, it was the tiniest yet most colourful and beautiful of servings. I'd gotten used to portions like this though, due to the restaurants that Schalk has taken me to all over the world.

"That's because I'm not the one that's pregnant, and that's sweetcorn panna cotta with crab cannelloni," I immediately felt the water that I had been drinking gush down the wrong pipe, while the other half that I had in my mouth went flying right out, landing directly on Schalk's face.

"Pregnant?!" I stammered in between vicious coughing and wheezing, clutching my chest and trying to see through blurry eyes. A server rushed to come and assist me, and just as he was about to put his hands on me to soothe my choking self, Schalk spoke up.

"Touch her, and you die, right now." His words were cold and cutting, his eyes on the young male server who looked at him with fearful eyes. The boy rushed to nod his head, bringing his hands back to his body and scrambling away from us.

I hadn't heard the interaction since I was still choking, I only came back to when I felt Schalk's hands on my shoulders, massaging me gently. Schalk brought a serviette to my lips, wiping at it and cleaning me up. He crouched down when he did that, his dark blue eyes directly on my own teary eyes. "Better?" he asked me and I couldn't even nod, I just looked at him.

"I'm not pregnant," I told him, my vice coming out wobbly and shaky. My voice was a whisper, so afraid of upsetting him but also the sunken feeling in the pits of my stomach at the realisation of possibly being pregnant with Schalk's child...what would that do? What would life be then? I couldn't be pregnant, not with this demons child. That would explain the constant sickness, the morning sickness that I'd been experiencing, vomiting every time I ate something or smelled something I didn't like a distant thought came to mind but I was fighting to push it away. "I-...I can't be pr-pre..." I couldn't even say the word aloud because I feared saying it would only make it true.

"Schal...Schalk I have-have my, my whole life ahead of me. I just-no-I..." I couldn't seem to gather my thoughts' together. Looking into those dark blue eyes that peered into mine, something told me he wasn't lying, I knew he wasn't lying. He'd been fucking me almost every day these past three weeks, cumming in me, never pulling out. I just, I just never thought that I'd actually fall pregnant...Oh God, I didn't think at all. I mean, even if I did, what was I going to do? Tell him to use protection? He would've never, and come to think of it, even if I told him, it probably would've upset him. And it wasn't like I was allowed to be out of his sight so I couldn't have even gotten a hold of morning after pills or contraceptives. I didn't think of any of that.

He cradled my face in his hand, his intense stare one that could suck out my soul and probably already had, "you're not saying you don't want to have my baby, are you, my soet Ivy?" he asked me, his voice having that cold with sweet tone combination, as if warning me of ever saying no to him. There was a dark glint in his eye, that one pitch black dot that grew and covered his whole eye if he got mad. I didn't want it to grow.

I blinked, feeling a tear slide out, my bottom lip quivering and my heart racing in fear of what he would do to me, "n-no, no, ne-never, Schalk…" I said breathlessly, my words coming out quick and afraid. You could hear the panic in it, hear the lies in it. No doubt he heard it as well, I wasn't a good actress.

He smiled however and leaned forward, pressing his lips to my own, "I'm so grateful for you babygirl, you're going to give me a child," he pressed his forehead to mine, "I can't imagine how perfect they'll be, because of how perfect you already are." His eyes continued to stare into mine as I struggled to hold in my cries, feeling my heart squeeze with every bit that he said to me. "You're going to be such a good mummy," he closed his eyes, placing his other hand on my stomach. I closed my eyes as well, unable to hold back the cries.

"Is…is that why yo-you br-brought me-me here?" I croaked out between wet lips and soaked cheeks and he chuckled, shaking his head.

"Well, since I'm already on my knees, I might as well," he pulled back from me. "Open your eyes, my soet Ivy. I want your eyes on me," I quickly opened them, doing whatever he pleased. I watched as he reached into his jacket and then pulled out a purple velvet box. "I brought you here for this, my soet Ivy…" I felt my heart slam against my chest as I watched him prop the box open, and reveal a diamond ring, "to ask…will you marry me?" and with that my heart suddenly stopped, the world around me fell apart and it felt like it all; stopped.

I looked at the ring, then at him, meeting those dark blue eyes as I wondered, God, what have I ever done to deserve this? Tell me, God! What? What?! How was I supposed to say no? Could I even say it? Of course not, this is Schalk that we're talking about. His eyes peering into mine seemed to read every thought and when I finally pulled away from my mind and focused on his eyes I swear I heard the voice of Botha warning me now, now…don't make us make you bleed, our Ivy…

My breath caught in the back of my throat and I tried to fight the sobs that were trying to make their way out of me, "y…yes…"

Chapter 17

"Turn left over there," I directed Schalk as I sat in the passenger seat of his Bentley Bentayga, feeling my stomach do somersaults as I watched the familiar neighbourhood that I'd grown up in. There was nothing like it, the kids paying in the street, the potholes that local governments promised to fix up but never did, the grannies standing at the gate with their hands on their hips, scolding the children to be careful of incoming cars, the groups of men loitering around their cars, boots open, cheap beers in hand, music blasting. Home.

"The beige house," I explained, unable to stay still in my seat as I reached for the seatbelt, clicking it out of place as I saw the wide open gate of my family home. "What the…" I trailed off at the sight of all of my family members at the gate, all the elderly women singing and ululating, my cousins dancing and kuku sweeping the street with a straw broom. I saw my father and my uncles, all singing as well, my father's side of the family was all over the place, singing the loudest, and all dressed in traditional Zulu clothing.

I looked to Schalk but he didn't look at me, he pulled the car into the midst of all of the chaos. Immediately, my family surrounded the car, continuing their singing and ululating. I watched as kuku danced the hardest from them all, tears in her eyes, as she stood by my door waiting for me to open it. I hated having all the attention on me and having so many eyes on me rendered me motionless as I sat puzzled in my seat. It was obvious that my family knew that there was a wedding.

At some point, I don't know when, I finally opened the door, surrounded completely by all of my family as they sang and danced for me, "ay ay ay! Setloholo sa ka!" (my grandchild) my grandmother praised, wrapping her arms around me and crying. "You've grown so much, my child. Today, you've made me the proudest grandmother in the world." She immediately went on to preach, facing everybody.

At this point the entire community had gathered and she began to shout in Sotho at the top of her voice, "I raised this child! I woke up early in the mornings, before the sun was even up, going to clinics with her, standing in long queues with my swollen feet and bad back! She took care of me, she was my baby, my child, and she loved me– still loves me too much! She did as she was supposed to do, she went to school and stayed away from boys! Her peers were falling pregnant left, right and centre, but not her, she held on to her education and finished school and she made me even happier when she went to university! And even then she didn't party, she stayed away from boys and studied and studied until she got a degree! For the first time in my life, I saw what a graduation was since I'd never seen such! There were white people everywhere," the crowd laughed at her words, some hooting and clapping as I stood beside her, her arms wrapped tightly around me.

"Today...today..." she began to sob, "She makes me even more proud! My grandchild is getting married, my people, my grandchild is getting married!" everyone began to ululate some more, people becoming overly joyous as I stood there unable to do anything other than be bashful under all of the attention. I'd been in this position before, not the position of getting married, but being one of the heads in the crowd. I remember when one of my other cousins were getting married, or when my aunt was getting married; the vibe and atmosphere in the air when you knew there was a wedding...there was nothing like it. I'd sing and dance like they all were right now. I'd ululate as loud as I could and do the absolute most, feeding off the energy of the people.

I watched as people did that for me.

"Come this side, Zama," kuku eagerly pulled my hand through her house that had been renovated with brand new furniture I was sure had cost a lot. The placed looked amazing, the walls of the outside of the home were glazed in gamazine, the once dusty yard was now covered in black paving, the once beige home was now a beautiful modern looking dark green house with aluminium windows, and an electric gate. Kuku pulled me into her bedroom and closed the door, setting me down on her new King sized bed. She'd owned a queen size bed before, one she'd bought 13 years ago. "soft, neh?" she said with a grin as I sat on the bed, feeling it, in awe of how things seemed to have changed in the three weeks that I'd been gone.

She sat down next to me, "oh, Zama," she addressed me, sounding so proud, "this man that you're marrying, what a great choice! I'm so proud of you, my baby. See, all that he's done for me. He even bought me a car, and now I have medical aid. Just yesterday an ambulance with a white man and a black man came to check on me, they were busy touching me and telling me they're checking what-what," she explained with glee and excitement. "I felt so important." I felt my heart squeeze at how happy she was.

I pressed a smile to my face, nodding my head, feeling the lump in my throat so I started to look around the room, "when did he do this?" I asked her, gesturing to the renovations. It'd been so long since I'd spoken in Sotho, my voice sounded foreign even to my own ears. Speaking English every day with Schalk had quickly become a norm.

You could still hear the excited crowd outside, especially with the truckload of groceries that Schalk had trailing behind us. If there was a way to impress an African black family, it was through food and money, and with the groceries that people were still unloading, there'd be no way that I could tell kuku that I wanted nothing to do with the millionaire that was currently being guarded by my father and his brothers like their lives depended on it.

"The second day you started working," she revealed and my neck snapped in her direction, my eyes wide.

"Eng?!" (What?!) I snapped in shock at her answer and she looked at me, taken aback.

She then nodded, "yeah...after your first day. The next day, I think it was a Thursday, I'm not too sure but, he came with some builders, they were drawing up plans and whatnot. He told me that you and him were going to get married, and all of that. What a good man you've got, you know, the neighbours are so jealous," she said with a grin as I sat there and then curled my hands into fists.

Oh my God, since my first day at work...this man has always had some kind of sick twisted plans for me. How the hell am I going to tell kuku that I want nothing to do with him?

I watched as kuku spoke excitedly about how everyone would talk about this and how she was a person among other people now, and that she was the talk of the church and everyone was so jealous, especially her rival, a lady from church named Doris who thought that she pissed lemonade-according to kuku of course. I watched numbly as she continued, speaking about how she'd gone to a tailor already and her dress was almost ready. I watched as she revealed that the wedding was going to be on the 12th of April, which was three weeks away. Even then, I didn't respond. It seemed there was a lot in my life going on that I didn't even know about.

I didn't know how I was going to reveal to her that I was pregnant since I found out last night. I didn't know how I was going to tell her that the man that everyone seemed to be looking at as a hero was instead the devil in disguise. How couldn't they see the horns coming out of his head? Or was my imagination that wild?

It was only then that tears began to escape me and I couldn't help it as I buried my face in my hands and cried. Kuku rushed to me, wrapping her arms around me and pulling me close to her as she kept muttering, 'don't cry, my child' 'don't cry'. It only made me cry harder because I realised how alone I was at the moment. No one would believe me even if I told them, maybe if I showed them my ear they'd believe me, but even then, what'll happen? Schalk was a powerful man, him and his family. The du Toit's had money, and I saw that now. His cousin was Heinrich du Toit, a man I didn't even know existed until a few nights ago at a braai that Schalk and I were hosting at his penthouse. Heinrich was the most sought out lawyer in the country and defended the most powerful of men in cases you'd never even heard of. His family had ties in the army, ties with the police, ties with the mob, you name it all; they had it.

I was just a girl, and he was a man.

Chapter 18

"**S**chalk-Schalk! Wait, no, no, please," I begged, gripping him by his shirt and throwing myself into his arms as he now stood in the garage, his convertible Bentley driver's door wide open. I'd chased him through the house, begging him to let me go with him, "Schalk, please, please," I begged him, my face buried in his chest, my arms wrapped around his body, "please let me go to work with you!" I repeated for the millionth time since we woke up.

Schalk was going back to work today and come hell or high waters, I was going with him. "I promise I won't leave your sight, I'll be right there. I won't talk to anyone, look at anyone," I promised him, needing so badly to leave the overly beautiful 5 bedroom 4.5 bathroom home in the exclusive suburb of Houghton. I needed to just be out of whatever space that was too Schalk, I'm not sure if that makes sense but it does for me.

When he got up this morning, I was already showered and dressed for the day. He looked at me and scoffed, laughing, before making me get undressed, get in the shower with him, and then come back out again. I had spaghetti legs after what happened in the shower, but I don't want to dwell on Schalk's sex appetite at this moment when I'm begging him to let me out of the house. "I have to go, babygirl," he said gently, placing a kiss to my forehead as if me asking to go with him to work was wishful thinking.

I pouted my lips feeling my spirit deflate. He wasn't going to let me come along...

"Schalk..." I decided to take a different approach, changing from pleading to a more sexual angle, "I promise I'll be a good girl...your good girl..." I said, letting my voice drop as I brought my body even closer to his if that was possible. I watched as his jaw ticked and I stood on the tips of my toes, keeping my eyes between his eyes and lips, bringing myself closer to him, "please, daddy," my voice was a dangerous whisper of temptation, even to my own ears as I closed the distance between us, taking his bottom lip between my teeth. "I'll be good," I let his lip go, instead sliding my tongue over his lips, taking my time in teasing him, "you know how I am when it comes to you..."

I slid my hand into the front of his pants, wrapping my hand around his member, cradling it as I've done so before. I knew that I was going to regret seducing him since whenever Schalk fucked me, it was as if he was doing it with the sole intention of making sure I wouldn't be able to walk. As it was at the moment, my legs weren't even working properly yet here I was, bringing him back to life. I finally wrapped my lips with his, kissing him like my life depended on it. His lips moved against mine and I felt him grip the back of my head, pressing my face to his as if he was trying to merge them into one. I let out a whimper, no matter how many times the man kissed me or fucked me, he managed to make me afraid each time.

He broke our lips apart and as I gulped for air, he turned me around, "hands on the car, babygirl," his voice came out deep and I bit my lip, ashamed of the wetness that pooled between my legs at his voice or how my body seemed to love the abuse that came from him. I put my hands on the car and he lifted the dress that I was wearing up, bunching it above my ass and at the arch of my back.

I let out a moan at the feel of his head at my entrance. It was a moan of pain, feeling his member at my already sensitive entrance. He slid it up and down my slit, my legs were wide open as he always wanted them to be. If I dared to close them, he'd sworn to snap them, and I believed him, so I didn't dare to close them no matter how long he abused me. "Oh...fuck..." I groaned at the feeling of him sliding his member inside me, stretching me even though I was so used to him.

Schalk gipped my hair in his fist, pulling my head back painfully, making me meet his eyes, as his other hand reached into the front of the dress, gripping my left boob in his head, and I let out cries of pain and pleasure at the feeling of him gripping it as if he was trying to rip it off my chest. "Schalk!" I cried out, my moans coming out choked and overwhelmed at the feeling of his cock inside me, stretching my walls, his balls slapping against my clit, his hand in my hair and his dirty voice in my ear.

"You're so tight, babygirl," he groaned in my ear, his voice when he was deep inside me caused my insides to squeeze and I felt myself cum. "You're already cumming, huh, babygirl? I haven't even started yet," he growled in my ear, slapping my face and pressing my body even further into the car.

My moans turned into frantic shouts at how rough he was, my body slammed into the body of the car with each thrust, the sound of skin slapping against skin seemed to be louder than my screams as he opened my legs even further, practically lifting my body off the ground. He pushed my face into the car and I felt my fingers claw at the expensive vehicle, "Scha- daddy- please..." I began to plead like I always do, "it's...it's-" I let out a deep groan at the feel of him deep inside me, probably all up in my intestines and tears escaped me as I tried to fight him.

"This is what you wanted," he slapped my ass so hard, I screamed, "now take it," he leaned down into my right ear, slowing his thrusts completely and doing a lone, long stroke that was so pleasurable I felt my eyes roll to the back of my head and incoherent sounds left my gaping mouth, "take...every...bit...of...it," he moaned into my ear, the sound of his voice sounding strained made me curl my toes and cum again. "That's it, babygirl..." he wrapped a hand around my throat and made me look at him as I came, "cream all over daddy's dick," he said, his twisted black eyes looking into my cross eyed ones that were dizzy with pure ecstasy. I hated it when he did that, when he made it hurt so bad and then suddenly made it feel so good...it drove me wild, and made my nipples so hard I was sure they'd fall off.

"Please?"

"No."

"Please..."

"No."

"Extra nice please with a cherry on the top?"

"Didn't you say you weren't going to leave my side?" Schalk reminded me as he glanced at me after looking at his laptop so long I was sure I'd become a part of his outfit. Schalk took it seriously when I said that I wasn't going to leave his side. I'd been sitting in his lap for hours now and I wanted so badly to get out of his office and stretch my legs.

I bit my lip, sighing, "I mean...yeah...but I've been here this whole time," I found myself complaining, a bit taken aback myself about my current attitude. I was always pouting and whining, Schalk didn't mind it though, I'd become very needy as well. "I just want to say hi to my co-workers, daddy..." I said leaning into him, placing a kiss to his cheek. He gave me a raised eyebrow look and then I laughed, "I mean, I won't leave. It's not like I can," I shrugged, "okay, okay, just give me 15 minutes. Let me say 'hey', 'how you guys doing?' 'Did you see the State of the Nation Address?' and I'll be right back."

He finally unwrapped his arm from around my body, "I'm only saying yes because I have work to do and you've been...on my case for an hour now. So you get 15 minutes and then you come back. We have a doctor's appointment in an hour and I'd like to get you home to change before then." I swallowed at the mention of the doctor, still having not fully realised that I was actually pregnant. I stood up from his lap, waving goodbye as I walked out of his office. I closed the door behind me and made my way down the hallway that I remember walking down for the first time in my life. It was about four weeks ago, when an intern had told me that Mr du Toit wanted to see me in his office, I thought I was about to get fired, but I ended up being force fed spaghetti by Schalk. I shivered at the memory, making my way to the lift and making my way to the employee's floor.

The moment those lift doors opened, my attitude changed completely and I was suddenly on the run, not even glancing at anyone as I rushed for Reeva's cubicle. I found her gossiping on the work phone and when I appeared behind her and gripped onto her shoulder, she jumped in surprise and whirled around to face me. Her eyes widened like she'd seen a ghost. "Ivy?!" she gasped in a shocked whisper, but I just grabbed her hand and dragged her to the bathroom.

We entered the female's bathroom and I closed the door behind us, making sure no one could enter by leaning against the door. My chest heaved up and down as she looked at me in pure shock. "I nee....I need your help!" I said to her in a whisper filled with anguish.

"I thought you were dead!" she suddenly snapped, "oh my God, where have you been?! What's going on?"

I tried to hold it back but seeing Reeva opened all the floodgates and before I knew it I was sobbing uncontrollably. I felt my knees give out from under me as I slid down the length of the door, releasing everything that I'd been feeling all these weeks. I remembered every little moment, every feeling, the way he'd stabbed my hand, the stench of Benny's remains, the feel of his kisses, his dark blue eyes; everything, and it all was so much. My cries came out desolate and anguished and even to my own ears they sounded like the cries of a grieving woman, so full of pain and horror, it was like I was looking at the dead body of a parent or a child that came from my own womb.

Reeva rushed towards me, trying to hold me in her arms but it was like I was melting in her arms, as if the tears that flowed out of me had turned my body into the fluid and there was no containing me. She still tried to hold me to her, tried to soothe me but there was nothing that she could do or say that could make me feel better.

"Alone...." I managed to say with a sob that bubbled out of me, my head pressed to the door as I tried to fight the sobs but they kept escaping me. "I feel so alone, Reeva," I finally revealed to her, and then and only then was she able to hold me.

"Oh, sweetie..." she said in a sympathetic voice, gripping me tighter, as if stopping me from escaping her arms. She held me close to her chest, pressing my face into her blouse and I lay there, receiving comfort that I hadn't felt in a long time. And suddenly I found myself crying some more at the realisation that it was a stranger who was providing me with comfort and not my own mother. I wish the chest I was pressed up against was my mother's or my father's, I wish that I was feeling their arms around me, encasing me in their warmth and safety, hearing the sound of their heartbeat.

But it wasn't...

Instead I was on the bathroom floor, a floor beneath the very man who'd hurt me, crying in the arms of a strange woman that I'd come to view as a saviour.

At the realisation that Schalk was still so close by, I looked up and gripped her hands, looking into her eyes with an indescribable panic, "Schalk...it was all Schalk, Reeva. You-you were right, he's crazy. He cut my palm, look," I showed her my hand, "and my ear and attached his." I turned the other way and she let out a horrid gasp at the sight of the two toned ear that greeted her. "He did that to me the day I came back from the brunch date that we had with you and your friends. It was Schalk! He killed Benny," I sobbed when I spoke of Benny, remembering the innocent life of a man I'd made the mistake of speaking to. My sobs seemed to be freed at that point, bubbling out of me, "he killed him because of me. He killed h-him, he-he p-put hi-hi-his bo-dy in buc-buck-kets, and then he-he...Reeva," I was inconsolable, "Reeva," I gripped onto her so tight my knuckles turned white, "please help me."

She looked distraught, afraid and in anguish as she looked at me. She'd been stuttering throughout my little speech, "oh...oh," she let out in heavy breaths as if she was trying to stop the racing of her own heart, her eyes showing the fear that I'm sure was reflected in my own and it was a sinking feeling, "oh Lord," she swallowed, seeming as if she was trying to get a hold of her bearings, as if the room was spinning around her. "We-we...we ha-have t-t-to get-get you out of there," she said to me, shooting to her feet. "Let's g-"

I looked at her absurd, "are you crazy?!" I whisper yelled, "He'll never let me out of this building. I can't just up and leave, Reeva, that's the whole point. I-I...oh my God, I don't know what to do...Reeva...I don't...I don't know what to do, or who to talk to, or where to go, or what's going to happen to me tomorrow. Re-Reeva...I'm..." I struggled to continue, falling silent as I willed myself to stop crying. "What...please...just help me. You're the only person I can turn to."

"Okay, okay," she began to pace, wrapping her arms around her midsection, "think, Reeva, think. Do you know where you're staying or is he keeping you locked up?" she suddenly asked, whirling around to face me. Her own cheeks red with panic and tears.

I nodded my head, "I kn-know where I-I'm st-staying. He bought a house for us, told me it was for us and our k-kids. It's in Houghton." She rolled her eyes.

"He's crazy, oh my God," she turned and began to pace again, "okay, we have to get you out of there. But how? I mean Houghton has constant security, knowing Schalk, you wouldn't be able to get out the front door if he had a say in it. We can't even get people to break into the house...Lord," she seemed to go off in a fury of words that I couldn't understand. Then she stopped her pacing, and then whirled around with so much energy I wondered how she didn't get whiplash, "poison!"

"What?" I asked confusion.

"Poison," she repeated, "we have to poison him, or drug him, or something. You can put it in his food or something and then just...just sit back and watch and then when he's choking you make a run for it," she explained to me and I looked at her, my heart racing against my chest, my mind spinning, my stomach twisting in nervous knots as I realised that this was what it came to. "Poison…" she repeated in a whisper, looking into my eyes with a determination I'd never seen before, with renewed hope and I felt it pull at me, making me see the vision. There was no way out, unless Schalk wasn't there.

"Poison…" I repeated, nodding my head slowly.

She nodded her head as if we had reached an agreement, "rat poison. That's it. That's the only shot."

Chapter 19

As I sat in the gynaecologist's office, every word that the doctor spoke as she and Schalk conversed had become like gibberish to me as I sat there, next to Schalk, physically, but mentally being miles away. I stared blankly at the corner of the brown desk that Dr Ahmed was sitting behind, the smell of a clinical room gnawing at my senses. I always hated going to the doctor, or going to the clinic. There was a smell that came with these places that I found extremely nauseating. It made me think of death for some reason. I hated those weird chairs you'd find in the doctor's office, except Dr Ahmed's chairs were fancier, more expensive, nothing like the generic office furniture you find. But those posters on the wall of wombs, cervices, pregnant women, and all things gynaecologist, glared right at me.

"...oit," I felt a gentle nudge from Schalk beside me and my eyes quickly shot from the table to Dr Ahmed who seemed like she'd been calling me for some time. I blinked, "Mrs du Toit, are you alright?" she asked me, her brown eyes looking into mine, her headscarf covering her hair, and she was dressed in what I knew was called an 'abaya' from the Muslim friends that I'd made on campus. Her white lab coat was thrown over the beautiful abaya, a black scarf covering her hair, a pair of rectangular glasses were on her face, and she looked like she was probably around her late 30's or early 40's.

I cleared my throat and nodded my head, suddenly pulling down the length of the skirt that I was wearing. I was dressed in a yellow wrap skirt with a white halter neck shirt. I felt self-conscious in front of the woman, feeling as though I was revealing too much skin and suddenly feeling ashamed. My arms were exposed, thigh out and legs showing, I wish Schalk had told me to cover up a bit.

Her assistant had already asked me to pee in a cup, and I'd done several tests, "well," she smiled at me, "I was asking you if you've been experiencing any symptoms?" she asked me and I could see Schalk in my peripheral vision.

I began to fiddle with the skirt, "well, erm, you know...not..." I paused, "not really..." I said in a whispered scoff. "I mean, you know, I vomited because of the smell of eggs these past couple of days, but really, I've been vomiting because of the smell for some time," I lied. The smell of eggs has never made me sick to my stomach, even thinking about eggs now, made me feel queasy. "I think it's just a bug I've come up with because of all of the foods that I was eating. I was travelling a lot, so I had a lot of food I'm just not used to. Raw food," I added, and she nodded her head, moving the pen across paper.

"So, you have been feeling sick? Vomiting, I mean," she further explained and I nodded my head hesitantly, watching as she continued to write down whatever it was. "And sometimes, do you find yourself waking up...not feeling your best, just plainly under the weather?" she asked me, and I knew she meant morning sickness but didn't want to deliberately say it out loud, because I guess she saw how I was deflecting and getting defensive. I almost sighed, and felt my shoulders fall, nodding my head in the most tiniest of nods, but I guess she saw it because I heard her resume writing it down.

"Have you been experiencing anything else?" she asked me, and I kept quiet, not wanting to say anything. After a few minutes of silence, Dr Ahmed spoke up again, "Ivy...I know that this might be difficult for you. It's nothing to be ashamed of, there are many women who experience various emotions when it comes to pregnancy. Pregnancy is a different experience with each woman, and with some it's more of a struggle than it would be for others. I'm here to tell you that you're in good hands. I'm here to make it easier for you, by making sure that you and the baby are healthy." She paused, setting the pen down and I looked up from the corner of the desk, trying to keep the tears out of my eyes as she made an expression like seeing me cry was making her sad. She stood from her place and walked around the desk, and wrapped her arms around me in a comforting hug.

"It's okay, Ivy." She cooed gently in my ear, "it's going to be alright..." she pulled away after a few moments and then presented a box of tissues and I thanked her under my breath. She walked back to her seat and then picked up her pen. "Okay, so," she tapped it on the pad, "you are pregnant, you're three and a half weeks along. Now, I need to know all about what you're experiencing and I need you to be honest with me so that we can track your progress, alright?" I nodded my head and she looked back down at the pad. "How are you breasts feeling? Are they swollen, painful, more sensitive?" she asked me, looking at me as I cleared my throat.

"They're more of sensitive and painful, not...not really swollen." I explained and she nodded her head.

"What about your mouth, do you have a metallic taste in it?" I shook my head no, and she continued, "Tiredness?" I shrugged, answering with a 'from time to time'. "Cravings?" I shook my head, "heightened sense of smell?" I shook it again, "frequent urination? Painful urination?" only after sex with Schalk was peeing extremely painful from my sensitive walls, but I shook my head. "Milky white pregnancy discharge from your vagina?"

"I mean, I had discharge once...like a week ago, I thought it was my period coming, but..." she nodded her head like she understood and continued on.

She asked me more questions and my answers were no. Dr Ahmed then told me how frequently we had to come see her and that she was going to be my gynaecologist until my birth and that this journey was going to be as smooth as she could make it. After an hour in her office, we stood up and made our way out.

I often found myself spending as much time as possible in the indoor pool, waddling through the water, floating on it, swooshing my feet side to side as I enjoyed the large body of water. Schalk had taught me how to swim, and at this point I was a pro. Before, the only swimming I did was when my family used to go to Warmbaths on the first of every Spring aka 'Summertime' and I'd cling onto the walls of the large adult swimming pool, doing nothing more than watching other people. I feared water and I hated being around it, but now it was the only time I felt truly at peace and calm.

Tonight, I wasn't alone. I was with Schalk, my naked legs around his naked waist as I rested my head on his shoulder, refusing to meet his eyes because I feared that he'd see the truth about Reeva and I. I still didn't know how I was going to do it so I chose not to think about it. I bit my lip, my eyes on the two toned ear, a piece of me attached to his. "Schalk..." I called softly, my voice like the soft flapping of a butterfly's wings. His one hand was under my ass, the other wrapped around my waist as he swam on his back, seeming to become one with the water.

"Babygirl."

"How do you feel now that you're turning 30 tomorrow?" I asked him, my fingers weaving through his hair, my eyes unable to break from his ear.

He just shrugged, "I feel normal," he chuckled, "am I sup-posed to feel something?" he asked me, and I nodded my head.

"You're turning the big three-oh, of course you should be feeling something." I argued with him.

"The only time I feel something is when it comes to you," he answered me and my fingers froze in his hair as I fell silent.

"Anything else, holds no importance to me. Not even myself." He added, his voice was painfully honest in that husky deep voice of his that had brought me so much pain, yet spoke so kindly to me at times, even kinder than I was to myself.

I bit my lip, bringing my head up from his shoulder and looked into his eyes, silent for more than a few minutes. "Schalk..." I swallowed, my eyes trailing from his eyes to his chest, seeing my name staring back at me boldly over his heart. Zama Ivy, right there, in big, untidy nervous black ink, seeming to take up all of the space on his top left breast. I found myself tracing over it, tracing the branding on his skin. "I wonder...wonder what life would've been like if, if...if we met like they do in the movies," I said, fingertips grazing over the mark of his life on his heart, wondering what was wrong with the man beneath me. "Maybe if we met at a park, or a library, or a café, or walking the streets Sandton, somewhere between the skyscrapers and the bars...and you bought me flowers-"

"I buy you flowers. I bought you three flower shops, one in New York, one in Florence, and the other in Hazelwood." He interrupted, not in a 'this is what I've done for you' but in a 'there's nothing less that I'd do for you'.

I continued as if uninterrupted as I thought of the man that I wish he was, "and you'd be kind, and soft, and atten- tive, listen to everything I say and remember all the small details. You'd drop me off at my front door, kiss me under the mistletoe, read out poetry to me, and make fun of the karaoke singers at a random karaoke bar that we'd go to.

You'd dance with me under the stars…your kisses would be soft, your touch one of a man written by a woman…"

"I don't just remember things about you, my soet Ivy. I know it all. I know that you blink a lot when you're lying, and I know that you hate wearing sandals because sand always gets in your shoe somehow and you don't know how it does. I know that you dance whenever any song plays even if you believe that you can't dance, yet I think nobody else in the world can dance better than you. I know you always say that you want flowers, but you don't know what to do with them once you have them. You don't know how much water to put in a vase, you don't know whether to leave them in the sun or if to put them in the shade, I know that you actually hate flowers because you hate the smell of them. Which is why, I've bought you plants instead. I know that you pretend to hate having tomatoes in your burger because of all of those prissy girls you used to hang around who'd go 'ewww, tomatoes'," he explained, revealing every aspect of me, pulling my brown eyes to his, and shocking me. No matter how well I thought that I might have learned Schalk, I know that I haven't.

"I'm always kind to you, babygirl and there's nothing that I wouldn't give to you. We share the same front door so if kissing you in front of it will make you feel better, then we can go there right now," I laughed and he chuckled, pressing his lips to my forehead. "I don't need to read out poetry to you, Ivy, not when I've got a walking definition of a love sonnet right beside me."

I closed my eyes, fighting the tears that threatened to fall. I pursed my lips, looking into dark blue eyes that I hated so badly for making me fall in love with them. I knew it a long time ago, the dark hole that I'd fallen into, the hole of loving a man as deranged as the man before me who'd made me cry so badly, I'm sure my screams still echoed the corners of the Earth, and the horror that I'd gone through because of his sick love was written among the most dull of stars. A tear slid down my cheek then, my eyes peering into his, expressing every bit of emotion that I felt for him, "...I wish I didn't..." I vaguely said to him, meaning I wish I didn't love you...

I swallowed, unable to stop the tears as he watched me silently, "I think I've lost my mind," I said with a pathetic laugh, shaking my head. "Because no matter how badly I want a man like I've described...I can't picture myself in anybody's arms besides yours." Was this what happened with your first love? I'd seen so many of my girlfriends fall for the wrong boy and get stuck up on him so badly, I got second hand embarrassment from the things that they'd excuse of the boy. I found it so foolish, so embarrassing, and so frustrating. Yet here I was...with a man far worse than any of theirs.

Schalk brought a wet hand up and wiped at my left cheek, "good," he said, placing a kiss to my lips, "because if you did, I'd kill the man." He deadpanned, no humour in his voice as if I was meant to feel the way that I was. "You're mine, my soet Ivy, and even in your mind, if there was another...I'd do unspeakable things to it." I felt a chill run down my spine, looking at the man before me, wondering what made him this way. There was no point in asking him, I knew all about

Schalk…all that he would tell me. He wasn't abused by his father, wasn't ill-treated by his mother, wasn't dropped on his head by a nurse, nothing. He was a normal boy, raised in wealth…he was simply, as he had said; a du Toit.

Chapter 20

I stood in the expansive third kitchen in the home, the kitchen that overlooked the Olympic pool and the horses in the distance, the statues of horses surrounding the yard and the beauty of the home that Schalk had bought for us. It was breath-taking, the kind of home that I'd had saved on my pinterest board, the kind of home I never thought I'd own, yet here I was.

I looked at the sandwich that I'd made for him, the fruit salad beside it, the yoghurt beside that for him to mix with the fruit salad just the way that he liked. His pack of Marlboro cigarettes on the corner of the plate and the cup of lemonade that I'd freshly squeezed and made, because I knew that he only drank lemonade in the morning. He wasn't a coffee or tea kind of man, he liked lemonade the 'zing' of it as he liked to say. He liked it to be sour, not too much sugar, just the way that he liked.

I rushed to wipe off the poison that had dropped onto the counter, using a dishcloth that I then tossed into the sink and opened the faucet on, rinsing it thoroughly. I closed the tap, standing there, trying to catch my breath. I gripped onto the edges of the farmhouse sink, my grip so tight, I feared it would break in my hold. I fought the sobs that wanted to escape, tried to grip my chest to soothe the racing of my heart, and the way that my knees wobbled under me. "Modimo..." (God) I called out to God, shutting my eyes as I prayed for Him to forgive me for what I was about to do. I wasn't a murderer, had never thought that someday I'd have put poison in anyone's food in order to kill them. "Ke kopa o mphe matla," (Please give me strength) I begged, my voice coming out wobbly.

I can't believe I just asked God to give me the strength to kill someone.

I took in several breaths, I have to do this. It's either him or me, and I can't live life like this. I can't continue on this way, so with that final thought, I straightened up, having delayed enough. I turned around and gripped the tray with both hands, making my way through the house, towards the bedroom. I didn't dare look down at the food that I carried, instead I looked far ahead, at where I was headed. I fought the tears that wanted to escape, fought the shaking hands, but it was no use. I wasn't a killer, and what I was about to do, I'd never thought I'd be able to ever do it in my life. I was a good person, I swear...but this couldn't be my life, not anymore.

I reached the bedroom door and then stood there for a second, taking in deep breaths and then, I let a smile appear on my face, letting it be bright and loud. I pushed the semi-ajar door and entered the room. I was met with the sight of the balloons that I'd been blowing up since an hour ago, before I started making breakfast. The room was covered in balloons, trying so hard to make his...final moments as special as possible. It was his birthday after all. "Happy Birthday Schalk!" I yelled at the top of my voice, causing the unmoving body in the bed to slowly lift his head from his pillow and look at me.

His dark blue eyes that were still sleepy looked around the room. He chuckled when he saw the balloons and me making my way towards him, "how did you get up before me and not wake me up?"

I walked around the bed towards him, before watching him as he sat up, "it was hard. I had to move an inch at a time, it took me fifteen minutes to get out of the bed and another fifteen to tiptoe out of the room." Schalk didn't let me out of his sight, and when I woke up, he usually did as well. It was a miracle how I had managed to sneak off to blow up all of these balloons and make him breakfast. "Here, I made you a sandwich, it's got lettuce, like you like, a little bit of butter, again, like you like, some cheese, polony," I explained the multiple layered sandwich where I'd repeated the form twice to give it the volume that he liked.

I climbed onto his lap, placing the tray between the two of us, "happy 30th Birthday, Schalk," I said with a smile. He was about to respond but he looked beside him, where he'd rested his head and there was a present that I'd placed in case he woke up before I got back into the room. "That's your birthday present." I explained to him watching as he reached for it and began to open it. I felt shy, "I mean, I didn't want to buy you anything, since you can get yourself anything you want." I explained the gift, watching as the gift wrap got less and less until he looked at the gift.

It was a canvas, with a painting of course. Not the 8 haired cat that I'd painted before but of him. It had taken me some time. I'd been working on it for about two weeks now. Through Schalk, I'd discovered my passion for painting, I always did it, always found myself before a canvas. I hadn't planned to give it to him as a present, I'd planned on keeping it to myself, throwing it or burning it. I'd spent so much time on it, spent so much time on creating the image of his face. It wasn't perfect, it wasn't a Picasso and clearly had its faults, but it was my best work yet. Especially those eyes, I'd never painted anything as well as I painted those eyes.

He looked at it, silent, "it's perfect, my soet Ivy," he answered me, leaning in and closing the distance between us with a kiss. I accepted the short yet gentle kiss, keeping my eyes closed even when he'd moved away.

"Again..." I called for him, needing to feel his lips on mine. I opened my eyes and grabbed his face, bringing him to me in another kiss. This time, I led it, moving his lips through mine, perfectly weaving them in a kiss that felt like the final goodbye. I dared not cry, feeling the way that he made my body come alive. I pulled away after what felt like forever and opened my eyes, peering into his dark blue ones for a moment before I chose to divert the topic of the solemn kiss. "Anyways, I'd been painting for some time." I explained the painting to him, "it felt right to give it to you..." I trailed off watching as he placed it on the pillow again, turning around to face me.

He coughed, uncontrollably, covering his mouth as I sat there, blinking in surprise at each cough, "you okay…?" I asked, feeling my eyes get glassy at how he appeared to be weak. I bit my lip and he nodded his head.

"I'm fine," he answered, he reached for the pack of cigarettes and took one out, placing it to his lips and I picked up his lighter, setting it to the cigarette and watching as the ends of it lit up. I was silent, withdrawing into my own mind as I reached for the fruit salad, dumping the yoghurt in it and mixing it up. I picked up a spoon, and began to eat it, keeping myself busy with that. "Thank you for this, my soet Ivy. This is better than any present anyone could ever give me," he placed a kiss to my forehead and reached for the sandwich.

I kept my eyes on the food that I was eating. I knew he wouldn't let me sit here and not feed me, so I kept my mouth busy with the untouched fruit salad, not looking up as I heard him take a bite of the sandwich and my toes clenched at the sound of his chewing silently and swallowing. I watched as he took two more bites and my grip around the spoon got tighter.

The process of poisoning Schalk had started since yesterday's breakfast. Reeva had gotten her hands on some rat poison after I'd left her and gone back to Schalk's office. Then, she placed the rat's poison behind the back tyre of Schalk's car, and I'd picked it up. When we were in the bathroom, she'd explained that it could take 12 hours if it was a large dosage, but usually takes 24 hours and more for it to take effect. I just had to keep feeding him the poison, she told me, and that's what I'd been doing. I'd been putting it in his food and drinks, including his Corona beer that he'd left in the fridge. It was taking a toll on him, he was sick, coughing a lot, wheezing whenever he did; it was painful. He could barely move at this point and I knew that this would be the final one with the amount that I'd put in the lemonade and the sandwich.

When he brought the cup to his lips and took four gulps, that's when tears began to slide down my face. He began to cough, gurgling, and struggling as he spilled the lemonade. I moved from his lap, watching as he coughed, covering his mouth with his hand and bringing out his fist to see blood on it. He gripped the sheet, seeming to need to rip it off him so he could stand but he was clearly struggling. I'd dropped my bowl some time as I was getting off his lap, scurrying towards the end of the bed as I watched on in fear. His nose began to bleed, his head falling from side to side and his breath sounded so short and painful. "I...Ivy..." he called in desperation, his voice coming out strained and in pain and I couldn't help the sob that escaped me at the sound.

"I'm sorry..." I cried, looking at him with flowing eyes and a breaking heart. It hurt me to see him like this. He turned his head in my direction, those dark blue eyes of his looking into my eyes with confusion, "I'm s-sorry," I repeated, watching as he fell on the bed face first, reaching his left hand out towards me. I began to shake my head, no, keeping my hands where they were as I watched him. "Sch...Schal..." I couldn't even say his name, as I slowly stood from the bed, looking at him with a broken heart, feeling every bit of me fight against what I was doing. A greater part of me wanted to stay back and help him, to call the doctor and get him to emergency care but another part of me reminded me of all that he had done to me.

"I'm sorry..." I kept repeating, my cries coming out pained as I watched him give me a disorientated look in those eyes of his that were so powerful once upon a time but were now fading.

"Doc-doc...t...or...." He let out, his body trembling as he suddenly threw up, throwing up yellow and blood and I stood there, watching him wilt and die before me.

"I...I love you, Schalk..." I said to him. Watching the pain that he was going through was unlike anything I'd experienced before. I don't know what I expected, but this was scary, so I found myself saying that I love him in order to soothe the pain that he was experiencing, even if it didn't help one bit. Then I looked at him one last time, terrified of what was happening and ran out of the room. I bolted down the stairs, still dressed in the lime satin shorts and the matching camisole, my hair in a bonnet. I rushed to the kitchen, grabbing the car keys of my Brabus G63 that Schalk had gifted me three weeks ago.

I didn't dare look behind me, tears falling down my face and landing on the floor as I threw open the garage door that was connected to the kitchen and entered the space where the three cars were parked, his Bentley Continental, Bentley Bentayga and my G63. I ran to my car, pulling out the phone that I'd hidden in the glove compartment. I dialled the number with shaky fingers, my other hand already on the steering wheel as I watched the garage door slowly roll up. "Reeva, I did it!" I let out in between terrified sobs as she picked up on the third ring.

"Okay, okay," she sounded as panicked as I was. "We're waiting for you, hurry!" I pressed on the accelerator and pulled out of that garage, speeding out of the long driveway that led to the majestic home that had cost tens of millions of Rands. I looked at the beautiful white cobblestone farmhouse home that looked to house the president, hiccupping as I thought of the man that I'd left dying in his bed on his birthday. I drove past the horses that he'd bought for me, drove past the Astroturf's, drove past it all as I reached the front gate. There was security there and I knew that they'd gotten instruction to never let me leave the premises, so there was no way that I was going to stop.

I pressed down on the accelerator, watching as the men yelled and jumped out of the way as I rammed the expensive vehicle through the gate, tyres screeching as I left a bunch of guards, yelling into their radios, probably for backup. I drove the car straight up the road, suddenly stopping it beside the stop sign. I didn't even cut the engine as a grey Polo GTI pulled up next to me. I threw the door open and threw my body right into the backseat of the car that had been perfectly lined to my door. Once one foot was inside the vehicle, the tyres screeched of the GTI and we were off.

"Fucking floor it Ricky!" Reeva yelled, and Ricky pressed on the accelerator even more than he was now. I sat in the back seat, trying to calm my sobs and my ragged breathing.

I buried my face in my hands, in disbelief that we'd actually did it. "It's okay, babe...." I heard Reeva's voice say to me in between my inconsolable sobs, "I know it's hard...but...you're free now..." her words weren't as comforting but hearing her say I was free almost brought a sad smile to my face.

Yes I was free, but at what cost?

Chapter 21

"Hey," came the words of a tired woman as I sat at the kitchen table, looking into the clear glass of water and the two tablets that I'd set in my palm. I didn't look up at the sound of the voice, my eyes more attracted to the old and worn table cloth covering the small round plastic table of the apartment in Botswana that Reeva had taken me to.

My voice came out as if spoken so far away, I wouldn't be found. "Hi." I responded with the same tiredness as hers did. I heard the sound of her slippers dragging along the floor, walking towards me. She pulled out the chair beside mine instead of the one across from me. She was silent for what felt like an eternity before I felt her place a hand over mine. "Does this make me a bad person?" I asked her, my voice still distant but there was a pain to my tone that I could imagine her wince at.

She brushed her thumb against the skin of my arm, soothing the goosebumps. "Not at all, Ivy–"

"Zama." I corrected, wanting to not hear my name from someone's lips ever again.

She quickly corrected herself, "–Zama. It doesn't make you a bad person, not a little bit, not at all. I need you to believe that." She leaned in closer, pulling her chair closer to me, her words going in one ear and out the other. I couldn't help the way that I was feeling. "Abortion doesn't make you a bad person and it doesn't make you a bad woman, Zama. This baby comes from a place of darkness, and this baby's from a person who never cared about your consent, never cared about you but themselves..." her words were true but again, I couldn't help the way that I was feeling.

It seems I couldn't stop being a murderer.

It was breaking my heart, looking at these two tablets that were going to end it all. The abortion tablets I'd asked Reeva to get for me at the doctor because I couldn't go myself. It seemed easier, and now she told me that it would take 1-4 hours for them to kick in and I'd lose the child. My first child...

It'd been my decision, in the few days that I'd been here, I realised that I wanted nothing tying me to the man that I'd left for dead. "It's hard," I finally let out in a wobbly voice, swallowing my tears and blinking my eyes as I turned to face her. "I hate that I'm going to lose the first child that I was going to have...and, and..." I couldn't stop the tears that flowed and the cries that followed, "I'd wanted it to be so special the first time I had a baby, and he's taken that away from me," Reeva pulled me into her arms, pressing my face into her shoulder as I cried.

She comforted me, rocking us back and forth slowly, she whispered, "it's going to be okay..." in my ear, her tone one of love and care that I'd only experienced a handful of times in my life. She seemed to always smell of her Chanel perfume, and even though I'd always hated Chanel perfumes, I'd become particularly fond of this one. Her hugs, her scent, everything, it made me feel like everything was going to be okay.

I sniffled, calming down a bit and then pulling my face away from her shoulder. I leaned back in the old plastic chair, "you've done so much for me, Reeva," I said with thick emotion in my voice, hiccupping as my other hand unconsciously made its way to my stomach where there wasn't even a bump as of yet, Dr Ahmed had said that I was going to show at week 12 of my pregnancy, most likely. It was still an early pregnancy so an abortion wasn't going to be as difficult. "You left your job, your home..." I thought about all that she'd done for me.

She smiled, "I can't just sit back and watch as a friend of mine goes through something as scary as that was." She explained, "And it's fine, Ricky had some contacts in Botswana, so it wasn't too much of a hassle. Besides, what's a few more weeks in Botswana for me? I'm going to stay with you until you get back on your feet. Ricky's already organised a job for you, so...you'll be okay, you'll be okay. It's a nice job, in corporate, nice little cubicle, smart casual work attire, no...no weirdo's, I promise."

I nodded my head, feeling my heart race in nerves at the whole thought of being left alone in a new country. I licked my lips, silent, as I reached for the glass of water and took it in my hand. I looked at the tablets and then put them on my tongue, placing the glass to my lips and drinking from it, swallowing the tablets that sealed my fate. "New beginnings," I said, pulling the glass of water away from my lips, "new country, new place," I looked around the apartment that didn't have any furniture because we'd come in here at the last moment, but Ricky had bought a nice and fancy couch and bean bag chairs for the living room, perfectly fitting into the two bedroom flat. "You...er...you heard anything yet from anyone at the office?" I asked her, finally letting myself ask her the question that had been eating at me.

She shook her head, pulling her knees to under her chin, "no. Actually, I cut all contact with everyone there. I threw my phone, emptied my flat, and called it a day. I think...I don't want to be in that environment anymore, and I don't want to be in that place or associated with any of those people."

"So, what are you and Ricky going to do after I've gotten on my feet? Where are you guys going to go?"

She shrugged, "I don't know really, we don't have it figured out as much as you do. Maybe Durban? Live by the ocean, get a nice flat there? I don't know, or Cape Town, it's just really expensive there. But the beaches are nice, restaurants are super cool too...so either one. I just like water, that's all." She laughed lightly, closing her eyes and then looking at me.

"You and Ricky are so...perfectly made for each other. I don't know many people who'd do what he's done for me," I began to play with my fingers nervously, wondering if the pain was going to be immediate. I wondered how painful this abortion was going to be, but I was glad that Reeva said she'd spend the day with me, and even more grateful that Ricky had left, leaving us alone for the day and would be back some time in the night. At least, I wouldn't go through it alone.

"He's just a good person, Zama, has a good heart, and wants to help people as much as he can. You're our friend, and he and I do whatever we can for our friends. You needed our help, and we were going to be there for you, in whichever way that was necessary."

"...thank you, Reeva."

She smiled at me, nodding her head, "anytime." She answered me.

I pursed my lips and swallowed, "I think I want to lay down for now," I told her, "be alone before...before the tablets kick in." I explained with a dry mouth and she nodded her head, her eyes shining at me with sympathy. I stood from the table, the plastic chair screeching on the tiled floors. I let out a long breath, walking away from the table before Reeva called me back.

"Zama."

"Yeah?" I asked, turning my head to look at her.

"I think you're the strongest person out here. You're more than what you went through, and more than what you're going through," she told me, her eyes shining into mine with earnest. "...you're not a bad person. You were with a bad person, you dealt with bad people, but you...you're not a bad person."

I nodded my head, lips still pursed, "...tell that to my heart, then." I turned and walked away, walking into my room and closing the door behind me.

Chapter 22

Today is the 11th of April, the day before my wedding.

It's been two weeks and a day since I escaped him, and 12 days since I aborted the baby.

The days are hard, the nights are restless, and sometimes I dream of him; dream of Schalk and his final moments. The way that he smiled at me, even though he was ill, experiencing organ failure, he still smiled at me and thanked me for the breakfast that was actually poison. I dream about how his nose bled, the way that his eyes turned bloodshot red, the way that his skin was patchy and slightly yellow, the way those dark blue eyes had looked on at me in strained agony as I kept saying 'sorry'.

Other nights, I dream of the way that his touch could be so gentle, dream of the way that he laughed whenever I painted something even though he'd promised me he'd never laugh at the art that I created. I dream of the way that he smirks, the way that he brings that cancer stick to his lips, the scent of his cologne and cigarette smoke still lingered on every parts of my skin; no matter how much I scrubbed.

During the days I experience cramps, as if I'm going through my abortion over and over again. I scream and clutch my stomach, cry and beg for God to help me with the pain. The pain is so great, I can't ignore it, I can't suddenly feel numb, and I simply feel all of it. Reeva took me to the doctor, he said that it was all in my head; turns out I'm torturing myself, the only question is which part is torturing which. Is my belly torturing my heart because I took life from it, is my mind torturing my body to remind me of the evil that never evades. Is it the soul of my unborn, murdered child that's haunting me? Asking me 'why, mummy, why? Why did you kill me?'

Some days when my stomach cramps I speak to it, speak to my belly, speak to my womb. I call on that child that will never be born, that will never breathe, and that will never know life. "Sweetheart..." I felt my voice call softly, in a broken whisper, tears running down my face, snot running down my nose, dirtying my mouth, coming between my parted lips and I tasted it.

I stood before the large wall to wall, floor to ceiling mirror. The dress that I'd been wearing was pooled at my feet on the floor, the shell lights above me casting an orange-ish light over me. I looked at my breasts, they were unmarked, unharmed, and there were no finger marks from how tightly Schalk gripped me, no bite marks all over my body.

I stood with my arms beside my body, looking at my flat stomach, "can you hear me?" I asked again, my voice becoming the most softest of whispers.

"I'm sorry..." I found myself saying, grimacing from the pain and suddenly gripping my stomach, my legs shaking from the cramps.

"Why did you do it?" it felt like she asked. It sounded so much like the little girl that I'd always dreamt of having. The kind of adorable yet smart kid who'd always have questions about every little thing that she saw. I began to cry, imagining my babygirl in a tutu, with her little curly hair and a toothless smile. She would've danced ballet, and The Little Mermaid was going to be her go to film, I would've named her something sweet and adorable, like Lily-Bloom. She'd one day ask me when she was teenager how could I give her such a silly name with a roll of her eyes because she'd think it was uncool since she's at that stage in her life, but I'd just cheese and tell her it was because she was about the sweetest little thing in my belly.

"Because," I paused, my cries heavy and pained, "because your father wasn't a good man, Lily-Bloom. I didn't want the memories...didn't want the pain that came with the past, the pain that came with keeping his DNA alive, through you. I'm sorry, Lily-Bloom...it breaks my heart, but I have to tell you that you had to go." It was hard saying that, but I knew that it had to be said, even if I only partially believed it myself. My mental state was deteriorating, I was experiencing things that my mind was creating and I was going crazy, getting crazier with each passing moment. I wasn't okay, but as

Reeva had been begging me for these days was for me to fight through my depression. That's what she called it, she called it depression, said that it drove people crazy and had driven her own mother to suicide and if I didn't get a handle on it, I was going to kill myself too.

I had to take a stand, but it was hard. I realised that I wasn't doing this for myself, but for her as well; for Lily-Bloom. "You're my mummy, you were supposed to save me," I heard her argue through another flash of cramps that crippled me and I let out a deep groan at the pain, falling to my knees and crawling into my body.

"I...know, sweetheart," I let out in a pained confession. "But mummy had to save herself first. I'm sorry, sweetheart, sorry that I didn't give you a chance... a shot at life. But I wasn't okay, and I wasn't going to be okay, even if you came. Your father, he messed me up, really bad, sweetheart. I don't think I'll ever be okay..." I swallowed, feeling the cramps subside, "I love you too much, Lily-Bloom, I love you more than anything, sweetheart. Look into my heart and you'll see the truth. It wasn't easy letting you go, it's still not easy but I had to do what I had to do. Because when you're around bad people, their badness rubs off on you, and you have to make decisions that not many people will understand. It's a lonely journey and you deserved to come into love, Lily-Bloom."

I looked at my stomach, my hands on it, gently caressing it as I felt the cramps subside. I let out a breath, "I had to let you go. I have to let you go, Lily-Bloom," I took in a deep breath, closing my eyes as I let the words out. "I've made my choice, sweetheart, and it doesn't have to be good, as long as it's mine…" I swallowed, wiping my tears and snot with the back of my hand, "…goodbye, Lily-Bloom…" to the girl who'd never come to be, my first angel that I'd had to let go of, my very first love, my very first child. I wish things had been different, that it was as I had dreamed it would be, but it wasn't.

But I guess that's okay too.

"Goodbye, mummy." Her voice croaked in a baby gentle voice that broke my head and I shut my eyes, placing a fist in my mouth to stop myself from sobbing uncontrollably.

There was a knock on the door, "excuse me, ma'am, are you okay in there?" the voice did little to break me out of the bubble that I was in. As I swallowed my cries and let out a loud hum in response because I didn't trust my voice. "Okay, do the clothes fit? If they don't, I do think that I got you a size bigger, here are some samples that are a smaller size."

I sniffled, in a haste to wipe my tears and snot as I stood to my feet. I cleared my throat and turned to the door, opening it just slightly and not revealing my face as I thanked the shop assistant and accepted the clothes that she placed in my hand.

I tapped my fingers on the steering wheel of the Mazda 3 that Ricky usually used as I turned up the familiar street of the apartment complex that we were staying in. I sang along to the music in the car, Ricky had left one of his Locnville CD's in the car, and I was listening to it. I reached for the ice tea bringing it to my lips and drinking from it as I enjoyed the feel of the air in the car. Today, had been a hard day, but, things were getting better because I was going to try and take control of my life. Schalk and the du Toit's had kept me captive for too long, I refused for me to do this to myself. I pulled up to the security gate, eyebrows furrowed in confusion at the absence of the guards, especially on a Friday. I simply shrugged, maybe they gave them the weekend off and I didn't know because I spent so much time in the apartment. Today had been the first time that I was outside and actually paying attention.

I drove the car through the wide open gate and entered the apartment complex, frowning as I looked around the completely empty parking lot. "What the hell...?" I whispered in confusion at the parking lot that looked like a complete ghost town. The apartment complex that we were staying in was large and had lots of families and people staying there, you could hear a thousand voices at every hour, including on weekends. I'd been here for two weeks, of course I knew it.

Maybe it's a public holiday or something? My mind tried to come up but I couldn't shake the feeling that something ominous was going on. It felt like I'd entered the set of a horror movie, to be quiet honest, the last time I felt like this was when I'd tried escaping Schalk's parents home the morning after he'd cut off my ear. At the thought of the man, my heart began to pound and my fingers began to shake so bad, I couldn't steer the car clearly. "Relax, Zama... He's gone, he's gone... you're okay," I said the mantra that I'd had to drill into my head, and Reeva and Ricky had joined me in reminding me my mantra.

I parked the car and reached into the passenger seat, grabbing the three plastic bags of the new clothing that I bought along with the Chicken Licken that I'd bought for

Reeva and Ricky as I turned off the car and climbed out. I closed the door with my foot, pressing the lock button with my top lip since I had the key between my teeth. I walked into the apartment complex, using the stairs to get to the third floor where our apartment was. With each step that I took there was a sudden sunken feeling in my stomach, getting worse and worse as I got closer to the door. I swallowed, feeling the hairs on my arms rise, feeling the goosebumps cause chills to down my spine, my knees began to wobble, my heart began to race; was I experiencing a heart attack? I was both confused and not confused at the same time.

My body was warning me of something, I knew it then, knew that what I was feeling was telling me that whatever I'd find, would be…something bad. I finally stood outside the silver painted door, my heart in my stomach, my eyes trying to see through the door. I stood in front of that door feeling like my feet were stuck to the ground.

Maybe Reeva and Ricky had packed up and left and when I walked in there I'd be met with an empty apartment?

They promised that they'd leave when I was doing okay though. I'm not doing okay yet and they know that too.

Don't be stupid, Zama. Do you think that they should stop their lives to accommodate you? How fucking selfish can you be? First you kill a man, then you kill your child, and now you expect those two people in there to kill themselves for you.

Stop it. Stop it!

From telling you the truth?

'Why? Why are you so cruel to me?' I asked my mind, 'I'm you, and you're me.'

I'm not cruel to you, Zama. You're cruel to yourself. We're one, what I say, is what you want to be said.

I don't want to open that door...something...it just...it's not right.

I wanted to turn and run, but I found myself extending the key towards the door and sliding it in, turning it. I gripped the door handle, my heart now in my throat as I slowly pushed the door open. As the door swung open with a squeak, I peered into the living room, since that was the first thing that I could see, and I found the TV on, playing some random soapie. I let out a breath of relief at finding nothing and then entered the place, closing the door behind me, "Reeva, Ric–" I dropped everything that I was holding as I suddenly met dark blue eyes that had been haunting me for weeks.

I stumbled back, falling into the door, my eyes as wide as saucers as I looked at a very much so alive Schalk sitting at the breakfast table in the kitchen. He wore a Nike sweater, his elbows on the table, his hands interlocked as he pressed his chin to them. His dark blue eyes held no darkness in them, it was almost like we'd been together all this time, as if he had expected me to be home at this time. I knew my face was deathly white as if I'd just seen a ghost, and a ghost indeed I saw.

"My soet Ivy..." he croaked, his voice so cold I'm certain it began snowing. He gestured towards the only other empty chair, right across from him. "Have a seat. We're," he gestured beside him at the two people I hadn't even noticed. Reeva was sitting on his right side, tears were flowing down her cheeks as she looked at me with wide eyes, an expression so terrified, I wondered what had happened. Ricky sat on the left side of Schalk, his face of even more indescribable horror, as if he'd seen the devil himself and peered into his eyes, and saw hell and the demons that lay within. Ricky's eyes were so wide, I was sure they'd fall out, his face so white, it was like blood had stopped flowing through his body, "having ourselves a little chat."

I began to sob too, realising what this meant. I wasn't seeing an apparition and this wasn't my mind playing tricks of me. Schalk was here and Schalk was alive. Seeing him now, I know that what's going to happen is going to be far beyond whatever I'd gone through. I sobbed uncontrollably as I approached the plastic table that was perfectly made for four, sitting down with wobbly legs, my eyes unable to break away from dark blue ones. As I sat he nodded his head in approval. "Would you care for some tea, coffee? Anybody feeling parched?" Schalk asked, looked around at all three of us.

All three of us were just crying, waiting for our sick and twisted fates form the devil himself. Nobody answered him, but it seemed like he expected that. He was silent, and then reached behind him, and I sucked in a breath, waiting for him to whip out a gun, but he pulled out his pack of Marlboro cigarettes. He brought the cigarette to his lip, and then produced his plain silver lighter that I'd brought to his lips many times before. We all watched him, sobbing individually because we knew that there was death waiting for us all. He took a deep pull and then exhaled, smoke releasing through his nostrils as he tossed the lighter onto the table right beside the Marlboro pack.

He then tapped his index finger to his lips twice, "okay, I think I figured out your little grand scheme. Now, feel free to chirp in and correct me," he began, looking directly at me, not once glancing at the others. "I think...I think this all started the day that I brought Ivy to the office with me, and if I remember correctly, Ivy asked me for 15 minutes to greet co-workers and some other rubbish. I believe that's when she went to Reeva, and they came up with an idea involving rat poison in order to ....escape?" he asked me, saying the word as if there had been no reason for me to escape as if it were all so silly, and we were a bunch of stupid kids.

I just cried, but he only nodded his head as if I'd spoke to him, "then Reeva gave you her phone to keep so that you'd remain in touch before she went to buy the rat poison, dropped it behind the back wheel of my car, Ivy picked it up, and brought it home. Ivy then put lethal doses of it in my food from the day before my birthday, and on the day of my birthday, my body collapsed from the deadly intake. At the same time as this was happening, Ricky had been making plans with his friends from Botswana and the Bonnie and Clyde next to me were ready to play hero, am I right?" he didn't wait for anyone to answer.

"As I was dying, Ivy ran out of the room, grabbed the car keys, called you to tell her that she did it, and then ran. She stopped at a stop sign and abandoned the car and hopped into you GTI and you were off. Then you got here, and Reeva went to the doctor for Ivy to get her abortion tablets, while

Ricky was sorting out a fake ID, fake license and degree and all that under a different name to get Ivy off the radar for me not to find her." He stopped speaking, and then breathed in his cigarette, his eyes on me, face blank as I began to sob even harder when he spoke about the abortion tablets.

I was dead. I knew I was.

"Anything else? Did I leave out anything? Okay, so it was the planning of the escape, the poisoning, the actual escape, the abortion of my first child...and...I think that's about it." He nodded his head, before he grinned, and then started slow clapping, "give yourselves a round of applause." He instructed, but none of us moved, we all just cried, "come on, round of applause," I was the first to do it, slowly bringing my hands up and clapping at the slow pace that he was, and Reeva joined next and then Ricky. "Good, good. You should be proud of yourselves," he spoke, stopping and bringing his hand to his cigarette, placing it back between his fingertips. "But now...now it's game over. Don't you think?"

He took in a deep breath, throwing his head back and remaining silent for minutes. We watched the slow burning of his cigarette as his head was arched back in the chair, his dirty blond hair in the air, swaying side to side, the smoke he breathed out coming out straight upwards as if trying to reach the heavens. He suddenly slammed his hands on the table, breaking the plastic thing, "It's game fucking over!" he yelled and we all screamed and jumped in shock and surprise at his sudden reaction. "Did you fucking dipshits think that I didn't know fuck-all about what you were fucking planning? Do I look like a fucking amateur to you motherfuckers?!" his voice boomed with a force I'd never heard before as I sat there heaving in between my sobs, terrified beyond what words could describe.

"You don't think I've had people poison me before? It's going to take a lot more than fucking rat poison to keep me down. You'd have better luck with a fucking shotgun down my fucking throat!" his voice was like booming thunder as his eyes glared into mine a darkness so sinister that made me want to grab the knife from the closest cupboard and stab it into my heart, killing myself before he could. "I am fucking Schalk du Toit! I don't die from fucking poison! Who the fuck did you think you were dealing with?!" his voice felt so strong and powerful, it felt like my eardrums were going to rupture. I gripped my ears, covering them with my hands as I sobbed uncontrollably.

He stood to his feet, pulling out a gun and grabbing Ricky by his shirt, placing the gun run into his mouth, knocking out his teeth due to the level of aggression he'd used. Reeva screamed at the top of her voice, "Ricky!" she screeched so hard I knew she'd probably screamed her throat raw. "Ricky!"

"Fucking look into my eyes, Ricky the fucking saviour! I'm fucking Schalk, the game master, the devil himself, the fuck-ing butcher!" I began to hyperventilate, sobbing so badly I was sure that I was going to send myself to a teary death at the ugly sobs that escaped me when I realised that this was just the beginning. Ricky was crying, tears like an endless river down his face as he looked into Schalk's eyes with a blood mouth and horror filled eyes. "I could end your life right fucking now, boy!" Schalk screamed into Ricky's face, making Ricky sob even harder.

Then his voice took a complete 180 degree turn as he spoke the next, "but I won't…" he let out in a calm voice, as if he hadn't been yelling before. "I'm not just a killer, Ricky boy, I'm an artist." He pulled the gun out of Ricky's mouth. He walked around the table towards me and I sat in my chair, looking into his dark blue eyes with great remorse as I sobbed, "how does it feel to see a ghost?" he whispered in my right ear, where his ear was connected to mine. I sobbed, unable to say anything else. He leaned away from my ear, now crouching at my feet. He spoke lowly, but loud enough for everyone to hear in the room.

"Ivy…Ivy…Ivy," he tusked, watching me with eyes so black they were like the abyss. "Look at your friends, take a good look at them. I've got a helicopter waiting for all three of us in the parking lot, it'll take us to the airport where we're going to make our way back home. When we get home, I'm going to torture your friends, badly. And then I'm going to kill them, slowly, brutally, you won't sleep for months, years. You'll need therapy, or even a gun to your head to escape their screams. And then, when morning comes…you're going to get dressed in that white gown, and we're going to get married. Don't worry, your turn will come too, my soet Ivy. I'm going to hurt you, so bad, so bad…you'll wish you shoved the rat poison down my mouth and slit my throat. I'm going to hurt you to the point where you'll know nothing but pain…" he watched me, the darkness in his swimming in a storm that was uncontrollable. "You took my child from me, Ivy, you took my mum's first grandchild from her...and for that, Ivy, there's no amount of pain that I can bring you that will ever please me."

Chapter 23

"— and united we shall stand," Schalk sang the South African national anthem as he walked past Ricky's dangling figure. Ricky was hung by his feet upside down, swinging side to side, and Reeva and I were strapped to separate chairs both looking on at Ricky. Schalk had stuffed a sock in my mouth, but Reeva's mouth was uncovered, "let us live and strive for freedom," he continued with a whistle to his singing as he pulled out his switchblade; the one that he'd used to cut off my ear. "In South Africa, our land!" he finished as he approached Ricky. We were in the stable where Schalk kept our horses and the stench was so strong, it made me sick to my stomach.

Schalk placed a hand on Ricky's head, "our anthem is really so beautiful," he commended, sifting through the different blades and settling on one that had smooth bits and jagged bits. He let out a breath, "well, let's get to it then. I'm going to start with you Ricky, so that Reeva can watch you die..." Schalk explained as Ricky began to sob and beg, but I knew that begging wouldn't get us anywhere at this point. Ricky hung naked, his arms behind his back, his body swinging to and fro, and he kept pissing on himself, making it run down his body and into his face. "Then, when you're dead," he gestured the knife to Reeva, "I'm going to kill Reeva, so that Ivy can watch her saviour die, and that's basically what's on the itinerary today," he explained as if he was speaking business.

Reeva screamed, "Please! Schalk! No! I'm sorry! No! No! Ricky!" Reeva was inconsolable and the sound of her pleas and her heartbreak was too much for my heart.

Schalk turned to face me slightly, only turning his head, looking at me from the side of his face, "don't look away, babygirl. Or else I'll slice your eyelids off, and you'll never be able to close your eyes again." Schalk's words pierced through my skin, piercing through Reeva's horror screams even if she didn't know what was going to happen. I sobbed uncontrollably, unable to make a sound as I sat there, feeling the soul crushing realisation that this was all my fault.

"No, please!" Ricky began to yell as Schalk approached him. "No, no! No- ahh!" Ricky's scream of agony met my ears, mixing with Reeva's shrill screams as Schalk began slicing at his member. I wanted to shut my eyes and look away as I was met with a bloody sight but my mind willed me not to, as the gory sight of a man's genitals being sliced off was unlike anything I'd ever seen.

Ricky's shrill screams were screechy, then deeper, then more anguished, then softer as if screaming took everything out of him. I was met with the sight of crimson flowing down his white skin, the endless flowing river that gushed from between his legs as Schalk sliced his balls, but only halfway, off, "now, what would be the fun in only slicing them off," Schalk paused before he gripped them and suddenly ripped them off, eliciting screams from all three of us, "when I could just rip them off?"

Schalk laughed as he looked at the balls in his hands. Then he walked towards Reeva who was tied to the chair, her arms tied behind the chair, her face a red so dark it looked like her face was going to combust. "Hold these for your boyfriend, won't you?" Schalk asked with a chuckle, placing them on her lap and then turning around, walking back to the man who was screaming at the top of his lungs, his screams coming out as though they were choking him. Reeva looked down into her lap, her eyes wide, mouth so wide open as it expelled screams so harsh and horrified I knew that I'd never forget them. I sobbed even harder, never tearing my eyes from anything that was happening even if all I wanted to do was look away.

"How does it feel to be a saviour, now, Ricky?" Schalk asked with a chuckle as he crouched down in front of the man's face, gripping Ricky's face in his hands that were filled with the blood from Ricky's balls. "Not so good, isn't it?" Schalk tusked, shaking his head. "Don't worry, Ricky, I'll let you breathe for now. I can't focus when your girlfriends making too much noise," he stood to his feet, about to walk away but faced Ricky with a smirk on his face, "she's a screamer, isn't she?" he chuckled, turning and walking back to Reeva.

"Thanks for holding these for your man, Reeva. You're a good girlfriend, you know that?" he asked her and she shook her head, her chin and lap covered in the vomit that had escaped her.

She sobbed, "pl-please, Mr du Toit! I'm so-sorry! Please, ple…" Schalk shook his head, picking up the balls that he'd placed in her lap.

"Open your mouth," he simply instructed and she closed her lips, realising what he was about to do as she cried so hard I wondered how she still had the voice since mine had gone a long time ago. She was still new to this, I suppose. "Open your mouth and eat these, or I'll open your mouth and shove them down your throat." Was all that he said and she sobbed, shaking her head.

"Please don't do that to me, Mr du Toit! I'm sorry! I didn't kn-know! Pleas–"

"Now," he shook his head, crouching down in front of her. "You didn't think of that when you told Ivy to poison me, did you?" he asked her and she continued to sob. Her broken eyes peering into his own as if she hadn't realised just how sick the man was. I wish I could scream and speak up for her, to defend her and make it easier. It was clear that they weren't going to make it out of this alive, but sitting here now, unable to do anything about it because they'd done what they'd done to help me, was the most helpless feeling in the world. His voice suddenly took on a pained acting tone, "what about me, Reeva?" he dropped his voice, sounding hurt, but it was clear to all of us that he was simply pretending, "what about what you made me swallow? You think it was easy, eating all that rat poison? It wasn't," he shook his head no, and she also shook her head no at his question, "it wasn't easy. I knew she was poisoning me, but because it was my sweet Ivy doing it, I let her. I let her feed me all of that, because I love her." He looked at me with those twisted blue eyes, conveying an emotion that made me realise that he was truly a psychopath.

"Don't you love Ricky?" he asked her, turning away from giving me his attention. She sobbed, not responding. When she didn't say anything, he stabbed the blade he'd used to slice Ricky's balls off into her knee, and she screamed. He used that moment to shove the balls into her mouth, sticking his hand inside and shoving them deep in there before he slammed her jaw shut along with her screams. "If you dare spit it out, I'll chop out his dick and shove it up your ass, Reeva. Don't fucking test me."

Reeva looked like she threw up in her mouth as her cheeks swelled and a mixture of red and thick creamy substance that was her vomit leaked from her lips, but she didn't dare spit it out. Schalk stood up and stretched his arms before he retrieved his knife, pulling it out of her knee and she threw her head back, gurgling through the vomit and the bloody balls in her mouth. My screams were muffled by the sock and my jaw hurt so bad, I was sure it was broken at this point. Schalk approached me, and as he covered the distance between us I screamed louder into the sock but the sock only swallowed them. He placed his hands on either side of the chair that I was in, "how's the front row seat?

You liking what I'm doing here?" he asked me, leaning in and placing a kiss to my forehead.

Now that he was closer to me, I could see Ricky's blood all over his face. I cried harder, "shh, shh, no need to be jealous. You'll get your turn," he told me, pulling his lips away from my face. He breathed in my scent, placing his face between my shoulders and face, sniffing my neck like he always did. "I ate poison for my Ivy, doesn't that prove my love to you, babygirl?" he whispered against my skin, his lips brushing against the sensitive skin and I couldn't help but only cry. It was the only thing that I could do; cry.

He placed a kiss to my neck, "I'm going to slice off Ricky's face and make it a mask," he chuckled, "you'll be surprised how easy it is to slice off a face, just watch this," Schalk commented in that deep voice of his that had reached me orgasms I couldn't count, and now it uttered things that I had prayed to never witness.

He stood up and looked away, walking back to Ricky. He crouched in front of Ricky's face and grabbed his face by his cheeks, "sit still, boy. I don't want to mess up the perfect mask." Ricky's shrill screams were unlike anything were like the licking flames of hell; they were death screams. He screamed and screamed in agony, as Schalk moved the blade carelessly through the surrounding of his face, outlining what he wanted sliced off, and then made his way inwards, peeling the skin off his face as Ricky's deathly screams went silent. All we could hear was the sickening sound of skin peeling off flesh– it was a disgusting sound– one that suddenly made me sick and I found myself throwing up in my own mouth.

Because of the sock in my mouth, the vomit had nowhere else to go except back down, which then collided head on with the bile still rising up my throat and then I began to choke, feeling the vomit escape through my nostrils. It burned so bad and I couldn't breathe, so I started to fight in my chair, suffocating myself. It felt like that was it, until I felt the sock being pulled out of my mouth and vomit escaped my mouth, flowing into my lap as I coughed and cried, letting out pathetic prayers from my lips.

"You don't get to die, just yet," Schalk spoke as I lay there, trying to catch my breath. "Now, soet Ivy, I'm going to call this the 'mask of shame' from now onwards," Schalk began as he crouched in front of me, holding Ricky's face in his hands. "It's almost like 'donkey of the week', so it's a pretty embarrassing thing, but...you know, that's that. Nothing you can do about it. Anyways, you've been bestowed it."

"N-no, no," my voice came out weak and meek, afraid and drunken because I was still trying to breathe. Schalk gripped my face as I started to fight, crying even more, begging him even if I knew how useless it was. He put Ricky's face to mine, and pulled out a stapler he must have gotten some time while I was choking on my own vomit. I let out screams as he stapled the face to the top of my hairline, then stapled the other part close to my left ear, the other close to my right ear, and the other right by my chin. The feel of the warm skin, the blood of it, the stickiness of it– it made me sick.

My screams came out horrified as I fought in my chair, trying to rip it off me. The stench of it was unlike anything I'd ever smelled before and it was directly on my face. "We'll keep that on until tomorrow. That's 12 hours from now..." he stood up and walked back to Reeva.

"Say 'ahh'," he said to her as if speaking to a child, and she sobbed, opening her mouth, revealing that there was nothing in her mouth. "You ate it all? Good girl," he said to her with a smile and then stood up, walking away from her and bringing back of big jug of a blue liquid, one that I was very familiar with. "Here, wash it down, Reeva." He told her as he stood in front of her again and she began to cry, her shoulders sunken and defeated as if she had no more strength to scream or beg. He crouched in front of her, bringing the large clear jug filled with rat poison to her lips, "I know you're thirsty Reeva," he told her, "look at all of this mess that you made all over yourself. Wash it down, Reeva, the same way you expected me to wash it down." He told her with a gentle smile.

"Pl...I-I...I'm-I'm..." her words came out broken and hoarse, sad and dead, "so-so...sorry...sorry..." she muttered weakly like she could no longer speak.

Schalk sliced one of her hands free, and placed the jug in that hand of hers. He patted his hand on her wounded knee, "drink it all, Reeva," he stood there and watched her, not at all moved by the poor state that she was in. He didn't say anything else and Reeva just cried, hiccupping as she picked up the jug with trembling hands, spilling the liquid all over her lap since it was filled to the very brim. Her sobs were broken as her eyes glanced at me, looking at me with an emotion I couldn't define; maybe hate, agony, fear, acceptance, despair, I don't know but her eyes were full of it. She brought it to her lips, sobbing, face so teary and filled with vomit, I couldn't recognise her. It was like I was looking at a stranger.

She brought the jug to her lips and took the first sip, a drop of it, Schalk stabbed his knife into her other knee and she screamed, "I said drink it all! Every last bit!" Schalk screamed in her face and she sobbed harder, nodding her head as he kept driving the knife deeper and deeper into her knee, swishing it side to side and she screamed, putting the jug to her lips and began to gulp it down, her screams mixing with the liquid into gurgles as she kept drinking it. She kept gulping it down, drinking more and more of it, the blue liquid spilling all over her chin, down her chest, into her lap, everywhere. She drank it to the point where she began to cough and choke and Schalk began to laugh, standing to his feet as he walked away from her.

I watched as the jug fell from her hand and she began to wheeze and heave the same way that he had. She'd taken so much of it, there was no way she'd last a minute more. I watched her body have an immediate reaction to it. She began to vomit, vomiting blue and red, her body convulsing in the chair that she was in, and painful gagging noises could be heard from her. Blood came out in thick clots from her mouth and her nose, and the sounds she was making were even more gruesome than Ricky's.

I cried, screamed and all, thrashing in my chair as I watched as Schalk started walking away, "Schalk no! Don't leave me! Don't leave me here! Schalk! Schalk!" my voice screeched at him listening to the sounds coming from Reeva as she was meeting her death, the swaying still-bleeding Ricky that dangled upside down, and the smell and feel of his skin on my face.

Chapter 24

I stood in the middle of my grandmother, my father, mother, Schalk, his mother, his father and his grandparents. They all posed with smiling faces and I couldn't even get my lips to nudge upwards. My cries were inconsolable, it was like I could still feel the skin of Ricky's face on my own, stapled on my face. I couldn't even stand to look any one his family in the eye, couldn't stand to watch the way that Schalk and my family seemed to get on so well.

I looked the most beautiful I've ever looked in my life, my wedding dress as if it had walked straight out of my dreams. At this point, I realised that Schalk knew everything about me. The dress was a white lace long sleeve bridal gown that was designed to make me feel elegant and beautiful in it. It was cut from the prettiest white floral lace, with a sweetheart neckline in a strapless silhouette, with a corsetry boning that cinched my figure for the tiniest waist. The mermaid skirt highlighted my curves with each of my movements, and the godet train added drama. The dress looked almost similar to Hailey Bieber's since I'd fallen in love with the design of it, after coming across the pictures on social media. My grandma had fallen to her knees when she saw me for the first time, and the expression on my father's face was one he tried to mask behind his Zulu manliness, but I knew that he was moved.

Today felt like the worst day of my life, the impending doom that awaited me after the ceremony was enough to make me sick to my stomach. The pain from the staples that'd been removed from my face only an hour before the ceremony still reminded me so much of the two individuals that I'd led to their deaths.

I pursed my lips, swallowing as I stood still in the midst of all of the chaos. The wedding guests who danced all around me as I stood in the middle of the dance floor, their figures only a blur, the music only a dull thump as Mi Casa performed live. It felt like the world was moving on around me, and I was just stuck. I blinked dully, the faces of the happy wedding guests only a blob in my eyes as my heart beat so slow, I was surprised that I could still breathe. It felt like I'd been standing there an eternity, standing in the middle of the dance floor as weddings passed, as if the guests had changed and the artists had changed from the award winning group Mi Casa to smaller bands, different couples getting married, man and woman, staring dotingly at the other. It felt like I experienced weddings in that exact same hall for decades, until I died– until it was the end of times.

And when it felt like I'd witness the signs of the end of times, my eyes collided head on with dark blue ones that'd made me this way. I watched on as my eyes focused on the figure that stood on the other end, the wedding guests dancing around him as well, passing in front of him, beside him, behind him, as if he were as invisible as I was. He looked good too in that white tuxedo that he was wearing, he looked like he'd put his best foot forward for this day.

Those dark blue eyes peered into mine with an intensity that didn't suffocate me, it wasn't that angry intensity of his, but rather a gentler one. Schalk wore his emotions on his sleeves when it came to me. I felt myself blink, feeling the lone hot tear that escaped my left eye, sliding down my cheek with the grace of a fallen soldier with no home to return to. I stood there, as he closed the distance between us, and I found it so sick and twisted that he could bring me so much pain yet look at me with a love that I knew he experienced wholly. His vows echoed in my mind. I'd been asked to repeat after the pastor, word for word, and Schalk had instead prepared vows.

"Ivy...Zama Ivy...my Ivy, my soet Ivy. I'm a man who always happens to know what to say, but today, you stand before me in your white dress in this venue with my family and your family, and I don't have any words. I can think of nothing perfect to say at this moment except what I'm feeling. They say the heart is a silly thing, it attaches us to people who are no good for us, and it attaches us to people who bring out either the best or the worst in us. There's a lot they say about the heart, but until now, I hadn't known what they meant. I'd gone through almost thirty years of my life, believing that this organ right here, had no other purpose other than to help me breathe. Today, as I stand before you, looking into those eyes...I realise that you've brought my heart to life. It gave me life, but it's never lived...my heart's never lived, not until...not until you..."

No matter how I sucked into whatever world I was in, Schalk always pulled me out of it. Schalk was the only one who anchored me to a reality that I both wanted to escape and never wanted to leave. Life with Schalk...it was hell. I hated him, hated him so much for all that he'd taken from me, and I know that he should hate me too. Hearing him say that, it made me cry so hard because I realised that there was nothing that anyone could do or say. I realised then, that his love was worse than his hate. Being loved by Schalk du Toit was a losing game.

He placed his hands on my waist, moving my body with a gentle side to side sway, completely to our own beat compared to what they were playing. My hands were by my sides because I didn't want to touch him, didn't want to even be near him. "This was such a perfect day," he told me, looking down at me and I kept my eyes on his chest. "You look better than I could've ever dreamed you'd look. Of all of the stars that shine in the sky, of all of the planets that line the universe, you, my soet Ivy, are worth every bit of my devotion." He leaned down and placed a kiss to my forehead, inches from my hurt skin and I winced slightly.

"...do you hate me?" I finally asked him, speaking for the second time today after saying my vows. My voice was scratchy and hoarse, evidence of the screaming I'd done into the dead of the night. I had screamed and screamed as Reeva died, screaming for God's mercy, praying for God to just end my life, praying for an escape, praying for a bullet to suddenly pierce the middle of my forehead.

I still didn't meet his eyes, keeping my eyes on his chest, "no." he answered shortly, responded quickly as if that wasn't at all what he felt for me.

"Why not?" I continued as quickly as he'd said the last syllable, "I tried to kill you, and I...I took the life of the child that you wanted, yet today, you have me here in front of you, in a wedding dress as you say all that you...all that you said to me. Why not? Why don't you hate me? How could you not hate me?" I added, feeling the back of my throat burn with tears as I looked up at him finally. "With all that you've done to me, how is that in anyway 'love'? Maybe, maybe you hate me, and you've simply misinterpreted the emotions as love." I tried to argue and he pressed his forehead to my own, closing his eyes.

"How could I hate the one who gave me life?" he asked me, breathing in deeply as if getting a whiff of me, every bit of me, and every essence. "I hate a lot of people, my soet Ivy, people who are in unmarked graves at the moment. My love is my love, Ivy, you're not just loved by Schalk du Toit, you're loved by Sakkie, you're loved by Ruan, and you're loved by Botha. Our love will be as we are, and that's different."

"I will never love you," I tried to say venomously, his forehead was still pressed to mine, a smirk stretched on his face as I watched his expression, not wanting to close my eyes.

"Whether you love me or hate me, doesn't make me feel any way, my soet Ivy. You're here to make me happy, not the other way around." He opened his eyes, those dark blue orbs staring into mine, "at the end of the day, you're here with me, and the rest of them...are all dead. You've got no one to turn to, no place to run...and that makes me very happy."

Chapter 25

The door to the room that I was trapped in opened and in walked a woman I wish my glare alone could send to the deepest darkest of hells. Rosita closed the door behind her, confidently strutting into the room dressed in a black Versace dress adorned in gold chains along the sweetheart neckline, her hair was pulled back into a low and tight bun, her face covered in make-up, and her lips looked fuller than the last time that I saw her and I knew that she'd gotten some work done on them. I looked away from her, mute, and looked to the side, looking at the door that she'd just walked through. I looked at the prosthetic legs that had been placed close to the door, exactly where I wouldn't be able to reach, and I wished that they could magically come to me.

"My, my," she tusked, placing her Versace purse on the edge of the custom massive bed that could probably seat more than 20 people comfortably. I was back in the bedroom that I'd watched Schalk die in, and the memories here made it hard for me to sleep. "What a sight you are," she scoffed, cackling lowly as her eyes regarded my pathetic state.

I ground my jaw, feeling my throat burn as I couldn't help but look down at myself again. I was met with the sight of my now crippled body, if I could say it was that. I was left on this bed by Schalk, and my legs were now a part of my past, a part of me I'd never get back because I dared to use them to get away from him. He didn't like that, and so, he told me that he was taking my privileges away from me.

"Schalk! Ple-please! No, no! Schalk!" I screamed at the top of my lungs as he approached me with the saw. After our wedding, he'd taken us to Peru for our honeymoon. We were on a private island, in a private villa, and there was nobody here to save me.

"Don't worry, babygirl. I have many Muslim friends, you know, I once went with one of my friends from university, his name was Muhammad. I tagged along with his family when they were going on what was called 'Umrah', fascinating thing, I tell you, my soet Ivy, Muslims are highly dedicated to their religion. Anyways, we land in a place called Medina, and there, we went shopping, walking along stalls and stores, and I realised something, there wasn't such a thing as closing their doors or locking their stores like anywhere else in the world. When it was time for prayer they would just drop everything as it was, leave it unguarded and go pray. I was fascinated," Schalk explained to me as he ran his fingers along the teeth of the saw. "Then, as we walked there was this place, where there were tens of beggars, speaking in Arabic and Muslim, I don't know how to say it. I noticed that these beggars were missing a couple of limbs, some didn't have hands because they were chopped off at their wrists, others didn't have until their elbows, and others didn't have feet until the ankles, and so on and so forth. Muhammad explained to me that according to Muslim law, when you catch a thief, you should cut off their hand to their wrist, and if they steal again, you cut off the other hand. So that explained why there was little to no existent crime there. The officials would cut off the hands of the thief and place their arm in this bowl or pot of boiling hot oil, and create this smooth finish around the severed part, making it easier to heal," he finished explaining, a grin spreading across his face.

"So, I've thought to do the same to you, my soet Ivy. Except I'm going to cut off your toes, and then dip your foot in the oil," he explained bringing a big pot of hot oil and I screamed, trying to fight on the steel table that he had me restrained to so that I couldn't fight him. I sobbed uncontrollably, my tongue unable to come up with the pleas to get me out of this. "Then, I'm going to let you breathe, because that will be punishment for poisoning me. Then, I'm going to saw off your feet until your ankles, and then dip what's left of it in hot oil again, make you feel burning oil and pain over and over again. That's for daring to use your feet for running away from me." He came closer to me, placing a kiss to my forehead and brushing my hair from my face as he peered down at me as I lay on the surgical table, sobbing and shaking my head side to side.

"Then the worst of all, I'm going to take the rest of your legs, bit by bit," he said lowly, venom seeping through his voice, "every hour, for killing my child. You will never walk again, my Ivy, you will never ever feel the sand in between your toes, you'll only walk," he leaned closer to me, those dark blue eyes of his glaring into my own with malice and hate that made me begin fighting against the restraints again, "when I allow you to. Now...sit back," he straightened up and walked around the table as I started to scream, trying to curl my toes inwards as if that would protect them, "I plan to make this torture last as long as you ran away from me. And that's fifteen days."

I only had until my mid-thigh, and at this point I couldn't even see it anymore due to my pregnant belly. I was 9 months pregnant, and due in 2 weeks. I'd spent most of my pregnancy in this bed, only leaving this room when Schalk allowed it. I was losing my mind, slipping into a strange place that I couldn't describe even if I tried.

"It's a good thing he fucked you when you were a cripple, so your little black ass didn't run off and try to kill this child," she mocked me as she approached me, a sinister look in her eyes as she snarled her lips in distaste at me. I looked into those eyes of hers and then glared into them, realising that I hated this woman more than I did Schalk. She used to be like me. Schalk had told me all about his mother and his father, how his father had taught his mother lessons, how his mother tried to run many times, including with them, and then his father, Mr Bertus had caught her and she'd paid for it so terribly, that she never disobeyed him again.

She was supposed to be helping me, she was supposed to be making me feel better because I was now in the position that she used to be in. Instead, she mocks me, "I wonder what this child will say when I tell it that its mother killed its sibling," she spat, her eyes as cold as winter, her face in a frown so ugly, I feared it'd be permanent. "You little bitch," she gripped my jaw and forced me to look up at her, even if I already was. Her thin fingers dug into my face, her nails cutting at my skin, "he trained you well, bitch." She spat, "that child you're carrying is my grandchild and you better make sure tha-" I didn't let her finish because I'd conjured up as much spit as I could have in the few seconds that the thought crossed my mind and spat in her face.

"Fuck you!" I snapped, feeling a fire course through my veins in an anger I'd never felt before. I didn't care what this would do to me, what Schalk would do to me if I disrespected his mother but I'd had enough of her taunting.

She looked at me in shock, her eyes wide as my spit landed on her nose and the top of her mouth. "You black bitch!" she screeched as she brought her hand back and slapped me hard, using her nails to scratch at my skin and hurt me further. I let out a grunt as my head snapped to the side, the side of my face she'd slapped burning as I ground my teeth, remaining silent. "You want to spit on my face, you filthy slut?!" she screeched. "You don't know who the fuck I am, Zama Ivy, I'm fucking Rosita du Toit, and you don't spit in my face." She glowered and I heard the sound of her storming away, grabbing her purse and slamming the door on her way out.

I kept silent, running my tongue along the bottom of my lips. After all the pain that I'd experienced at the hands of her son, this slap felt like nothing. If anything, I tried to bite back a laugh. I sat up straight, adjusting the large pregnant lady pillow that Schalk had bought for me that I never tore myself away from because of how comfortable it felt. I looked at the TV, watching the movie The Harder They Fall and admiring how well Regina King played a villain.

Schalk had gone to buy me ice-cream, an ice-cream that I'd tasted once back in May last year, in Cape Town, from a really cute ice-cream shop. I wanted the exact same ice-cream that I had then, and forced him to go get it. He'd called an hour ago, telling me that he was on the way back and would be here in the hour, so I'd prepared myself. When he walked through the door, I sniffled, acting as though I'd been crying by wiping my tears quickly and looking up at him with a sad smile and red rimmed eyes.

He closed the door behind him, holding the ice-cream that I'd been lissing for since 7:00 today. He furrowed his brows as he approached me, his eyes immediately on my face as I 'tried' to hide the marks that his mother had left on my face. If there was one thing that I knew about Schalk was that he'd never let anyone lay a hand on me, mother or not, and Rosita had crossed a line that I knew she'd never be able to uncross. "Who did this to you?" he asked me, setting the ice cream on my lap, and then gently gripping my face and making me look up at him. He brushed my hair to the side, and then gently slid the pad of his thumb over the swollen cheek with the nail marks.

I bit my lip, evading his eyes and speaking lowly, "R...Rosita. She came in earlier and then, she just, started saying all of these nasty things to me," I began, feeling the back of my throat clog up, the tears burning behind my eyes and my voice becoming wobbly. "I wasn't giving her any attention and then she just, she just attacked me." I brought my hand to my mouth, trying to stifle my cries, "she called me, a, a...black bitch." I revealed, and he pulled me into his chest, running a hand down my back and comforting me.

His big arms around me provided me with a comfort that I hated feeling at times, but I never refused. He made me feel like he could save me from even my thoughts themselves– as if he'd never hurt me, and he was my shield. I knew better, my memories and nightmares, and my now non-existent legs reminded me so much of the torture that he'd put me through. Schalk was a sick man, one that I'd become attached to. One that I'd learned so well in the time that I'd spent in this room.

The tears didn't stop flowing, not because of what Rosita had called me or what she'd done to me. Her words meant nothing to me, her touch was like the gentle kiss of a butterfly– it was the way that I both hated and loved the man that I was married to. I cried like this because I realised how sad my life was, how alone I was, how Schalk owned me, mentally, physically, emotionally. He owned every part of me, and he took what he pleased and never gave it back.

He'd taken the best of me, and no matter how terrible he was, how much of a bad person he was, he still continued to live a happy life. He had all that he wanted, the money, me. I'd been a good person, yet look at me, here, in his arms, being his toy.

I'd stopped praying a long time ago, but only now did I realise the absence of God in my life, and I knew then, I'd never believe in anything else ever again.

Chapter 26

I felt an anger burning through the very front of my brain, my hands clenching and unclenching around the cigarette and lighter, as I stared at the box of Marlboro cigarettes and the silver lighter. I swallowed, each time that I blinked, I saw my wife's perfect face marred with the scratches that my mother put on her. My mother had always been my number one, there was no woman that I loved more than her, no woman that I was devoted to more than her, no woman that I respected more than her, until now. My Ivy came first, always.

"Son..." I heard her voice call out to me in a soft toned voice as she walked into the kitchen of her home. I didn't look up at her, didn't need to. I had the ability to study people and memorise every bit of their movements, actions, thoughts, it was an ability I couldn't explain, and I guess I picked it up form simply being a du Toit. I knew that she wrapped her silk gown tighter around her waist and crossed her arms under her chest, I knew that she was looking at me in question because I was at my childhood home and not at my home with Ivy, taking care of her as I've been doing. "Would you like a cup of coffee, tea, or some lemonade?" she asked me, walking closer towards me and placing a hand on my shoulder.

I didn't answer her, instead she looked on at the table at what I was looking at. "I promised Ivy I'd stop smoking for her, and for the baby," I repeated. My mother already knew this, I hadn't smoked in three months, and it was the longest and hardest three months of my life, but I had to get healthier, for Ivy and for our future children. I used to smoke a pack a day, and right now, as I looked at the Marlboro pack of cigarettes, my fingers tingled at the familiar feel of the 'cancer stick' as Ivy calls it, between them, the feel of the toxic smoke filling up my lungs, the cold feel of the silver lighter.

I missed it.

Don't do it Sakkie came through, his voice encouraging me to do whatever to make our pregnant wife happy. Sakkie was head over heels for Ivy, wore his heart on his sleeve, was willing to do anything to please her and put a smile on her face. He was the most smitten from the four of us, no more smoking, Schalk. For Ivy. We have to be better, for Ivy.

You're focusing on the wrong thing, Schalk, Botha came through, his smooth and calm voice seeping past Sakkie's one. Ma's touched Ivy, and she needs to be a taught a lesson. She called her a black bitch, slice her tongue and shove it down her throat. She's overstepped her boundaries, and now...we unfortunately have to make her pay. Pull out the mask of shame.

I did as he said and pulled out the mask of shame that I'd had in my pocket. I unfolded the skin of Ricky boy, smiling at the memory of how amazing that day was. Ricky boy and Reeva were the first unmarked graves in my new home with my darling Ivy. Sometimes, I'd wake up in the middle of the night to her crying, looking outside our bedroom balcony into the graveyard that was actually just a levelled and cleaned patch of land, and obviously remembering me digging the shallow graves of her friends.

"Ma, I'm afraid you already know why I'm here," I began, smoothing out the mask onto the table and slowly lifting my head to meet the eyes that belonged to a woman that I'd never stop loving. I loved my mother dearly, and the fact that I was willing to teach her a lesson proved that.

Her eyes widened and she looked at me with a shocked expression, "what are you talking about, my child?" she asked me, her eyebrows furrowed, a frown deep on her lips, "I'm...I'm your mother. I gave birth to you, you don't come here and try to teach me a lesson. Is that what this is about?" her voice got louder as she looked at me with betrayal swimming deep in her eyes.

"You crossed the line, ma." I answered, simply, my voice low, calm and collected while she began to lose her cool.

"What do you mean, I crossed the line, Schalk?! I'm your fucking mother! I don't cross any line. You don't teach me lessons, I'm not one of your women! What's gotten into you? You'd never do this to me!" she began to shout, slamming her hands on the table and grabbing the pack of cigarettes and squeezing it in her hands as she glared at me. "This here," she gestured towards it and the lighter, "this is you! This is Schalk, not this man who stands in front of me telling me that I've crossed the line." She threw the pack of cigarettes in my face, but I hadn't moved.

Doesn't she know that even the best of people change? Botha chimed, his voice one of boredom at this point, wisdom in his words however.

You're taking too fucking long Botha and Schalk, teach her the lesson already! She doesn't get to hurt my wife and think that she's above it! She needs to know and she needs to know now! Ruan snapped, his voice cold and impatient.

Patience, Ruan, let's watch her crumble. There's beauty in chaos...

"Wh..." my mother calmed, watching me, her eyes seeming to look on at me as though she were looking at a stranger, "what...what's gotten into you? What-what's happened to you?" she asked me, her voice now low and sad, as if she didn't recognise the person that I was before her. I remained silent, letting her say whatever she needed to get off her chest. "She's changed you, turned you...against me."

I hadn't changed, I was still the same person that I'd always been; my heart just had space for another. My mother hated not having control, she hated that I was slipping out of her grasp and this was making her lash out like this. I finally decided to speak, "bring me your hand," I told her, instructing her, "I plan to take the fingers you used to scratch her face, and the tongue you used when you swore her," I then gestured towards the mask, "on top of that, I'm going to stitch this mask of shame on your face, and then I'll be on my way." I explained simply to her.

She stared at me, clenching her jaw and swallowing, "you do know what this will do to the family, right? Your father...Schalk, he won't let you get away with this." She looked at me, her words the final bullet that she'd hurl at me, but they didn't affect me. She'd touched my wife, touched what was mine and I wasn't going to let her just walk away. If it was anybody else, they'd be begging for me to kill them right now, but she was my mother, so I wouldn't teach her for too long.

I didn't answer, I simply picked up the lighter, planning on burning her fingers off. "Let's get this lesson started with, ma."

She turned and ran and I watched after her, I tried to stop my chuckle, but a bright grin spread across my face at the fact that she was giving me a little chase. "Damn, this is going to be fun," I said with a chuckle, standing from the chair, grabbing the mask and the lighter as I whistled, and following after her.

I walked back into the bedroom, finding my wife looking over the baby toys that we'd gone out and bought a couple weeks ago. I found her doing things like this a lot of the time, especially now that her due date was drawing closer. I knew that she couldn't wait to meet our daughter and I found myself picturing what our daughter would look like. Would she look like my sweet Ivy, or like me, or the both of us? Her eyes, would they be round, hooded or almond shaped? What would her smile make me feel? Her tiny feet, tiny hands, her laugh, oh, what would her laugh sound like?

Probably like heaven Botha chuckled, the four of us overjoyed at the realisation that we were going to become fathers in a matter of a few days. She's going to be perfect, because Ivy's perfect.

Yeah, Ruan agreed I can't wait to teach her how to ride a bicycle. Ivy said she wanted her to do ballet, imagine her wearing a tutu and twirling, doing that pirouette. Oh she's going to be perfect.

Ivy noticed me then and looked up at me, "Schalk?" she called in question as I approached her. She looked over my appearance, "you're covered in blood." She simply stated as if she was used to it, as if me being covered in it was simply some fashion statement.

"It's my mother's" I revealed, presenting my hand to her where three digits of fingers that were hidden in my palm. The fingers were black and burned, and they smelled too, "these are the fingers that scratched your skin," I handed them to her, needing her to accept that there'd be no one nor anything that could ever harm her as long as I had something to do with it. She was my darling Ivy, and nobody would ever hurt her, nobody would ever make her feel unsafe, not unless it was me and it was a part of her lessons.

She looked at them and then at me. She brought her hand out and I smiled, placing them in her own palm and she looked at them, her face one of fear. "You...you..." she stammered and then trailed off, not saying anything.

"Nobody will ever lay a hand on your, my soet Ivy, nobody will ever hurt you, or say anything hurtful to you. It doesn't matter who they are, they'll be dealt with." I explained as I stepped back from her and removed my shirt tossing it over my shoulder.

"Schalk?" she called again and I hummed, slipping my feet out of the boots that I was wearing. "Can I ask you something?" she asked me and I hummed, nodding my head. She cleared her throat and I lifted my head and looked at her, watching the way that she looked at me nervously. "The, erm...the voices in your head, Ruan, Botha and Sakkie, do they, like," she seemed nervous and I blinked, waiting to see what she was trying to say, "talk, like out loud?"

I raised a brow, walking towards the bed, "talk aloud, how?" I asked as I climbed under the covers. I'd been explaining Ruan, Botha and Sakkie to her for months now. I knew that she found it both scary and interesting. She seemed to be nervous to ask about them whenever she managed to, she stuttered a lot and tried to brush it off. I knew she wanted to ask more but I wasn't going to push her. If she wanted to know, she'd have to have the guts to say something.

"Like, if I were to ask you if I could speak to one of them, would they answer me?" she asked, biting her bottom lip as she felt my eyes on her face.

I nodded, "they would."

"So if I said, 'hey, Sakkie', would his answer come out of your mouth, or would it only be in your head?" she explained and I realised what she was trying to say.

Hello, my Ivy, Sakkie grinned, happiness and giddiness through every word.

"He'll answer, but only in my head, and then I'll say it." I paused, "Sakkie says hello, my Ivy." She smiled and then laughed, shaking her head. I watched as she turned and threw ma's fingers on the bed side table on either before she turned to face me, her face excited.

"That's...actually...it's both crazy and cool," she admitted, tucking a strand behind her right ear that I knew she hated showing to the outside world because she hated that I'd attached my ear to hers. She always covered it by keeping her hair down, but I didn't say anything, choosing for her to do as she pleased with the scars that I'd given her. I never hid my ear though, never felt the need to. "Okay," she nodded her head, a smile spreading across her now swollen face from the pregnancy, "can I talk to Sakkie?" she asked me.

Of course, my Ivy...you don't even need to ask.

"Of course, you don't even need to ask," I repeated.

"Hi, Sakkie," she said nervously, looking into my eyes, and I could almost feel Sakkie purr at the sound of her calling his name.

Oh, my Ivy. If ever God allowed us to hear a glimpse of what angels in heaven sounded like as those heavenly gates opened, your voice would be it.

"Erm, it's nice to speak to you, finally." Ivy spoke awkwardly as her eyes tried to look away from mine, and then looked back, and then looked away because she couldn't stand to look at me for too long. "My name's Ivy, but I know you already know that, duh. That's so stupid, dammit, why am I being so stupid?" she started to talk to herself, shaking her head. "okay, okay...Sakkie, I don't know what to say to you, really, since this is a bit weird for me because Schalk's giving me that blank stare of his-"

Sakkie chuckled, yeah, he has that stupid blank stare that he always does. Would a smile kill him?

I repeated the words and she laughed, "So Sakkie, I hear you're smitten with me..."

Smitten doesn't even begin to describe it.

"How does it feel now that you're going to be a father? Now that you're all...all going to become fathers, do I say it like that?" she asked hesitantly.

The fact that you're carrying a part of us, with a part of you, and you'll bring the perfect combination of us and you into this world in days...it feels like everything's going to make sense. It feels like it does loving you, it feels like we're only going to start living then.

I repeated the words and she fell silent, her face twisted in emotion as she looked into my eyes as if she wasn't seeing me anymore but seeing Sakkie before her. She nodded her head, pursing her lips as she tried to stop the tears, "thank you, Sakkie. You really are the poet that Schalk says you are. Maybe even..." she fell silent, her eyes looking between my two eyes as if the illusion of Sakkie she thought she saw had now disappeared, "maybe even the best part of him, if I could say," she spoke lowly.

Sakkie was silent for a bit, I'm here, my Ivy, always will be. I'm a part of Schalk, look into his eyes...look at me, Ivy...see me...

She peered back into my eyes, hearing the words, her brown orbs searching my own for the image of the man that spoke in poetry to her, the 'better' part of me that I know she wished would've been who was standing before her. "I do, Sakkie, I see you, but not for long. You keep slipping away..."

Sakkie was silent at that because he knew it was true. They existed in my mind, experiencing what I experienced. There was no seeing them, and I don't know if Ivy knew that, knew that she was seeing what she wanted to see in my eyes and not what was actually there. However, our love for Ivy was different, Sakkie's love for her was softer than the rest of the others, Botha's love was more mature but measured, and Ruan's love was angry, I, on the other hand, felt all of their love for her, while they only experienced one part of it.

Hearing the silence from Sakkie, feeling the heartbreak that came from the realisation that he would always be trapped in my mind, loving her yet never getting the chance to love her was enough to make me realise that with loving my sweet Ivy, came a tug of war with myself and my mind on who could actually have the pleasure of being loved by her.

They all wanted to be loved, but she'd always say Schalk, and never their names, and that's why I knew that they all retreated away, disappearing away from my mind as Ivy kept peering into my eyes, searching for Sakkie but he was already gone.

"He's gone," I revealed to her and I watched the way that her face fell, but she nodded, okay. "You can talk to him another time, talk to Botha, Ruan," I explained, pulling her body closer to mine and pressing a kiss to her temple.

"Yeah…" she answered, pressing her face into my chest as I wrapped my arms tighter around her, realising that this was one of the last few days that would be just the two of us, and that it would never be like this ever again. I pressed my nose to her hair, staying wide awake in the dark as she snored softly and I sat there, soaking in every moment.

Epilogue

Today was the day of the arrival of the next generation of du Toit's, a day that signified a great change in the lineage of the pure blooded Afrikaans family. The weather was cold and gloomy, even though it was summer in January, the clouds were thick and black, birds hid in their nests, hiding their faces in their puffed out necks, the trees swayed side to side, as if in tune to a sad hymn of what was happening. Encouraging doctors who yelled, "Push! Keep pushing!" and the horrid and pained screeches that came from a woman bringing into the world yet another gift, yet another du Toit.

"Who is she?" came the voice of a woman who too, once was in the position of the woman behind the closed door where several doctors and nurses attended to the birth. Rosita du Toit had once been in the same position as the younger Ivy was, and she remembered each of her births because of how long and treacherous the labour was. She'd been in labour for 18 hours with Johannes, her first born, and 36 hours with her second born Schalk. She'd pushed the memory of labour to the very back of her mind, curled it up and folded it with the memories of what her husband had done to her and all those lessons she'd been taught.

Today, she gripped the Birkin bag tighter in her left hand, her right hand covered in a bloody bandage as she stood, glowering at the man who sat in one of the waiting chairs in the waiting room of the private hospital. Her husband, Bertus du Toit, sat in his Armani suit, leg crossed over his knee as he drank a cup of coffee due to the harsh weather. He had on a pair of reading glasses since he was reading over some contracts, before his wife stormed into the waiting room, heading straight for him.

Bertus lifted his head to look at the woman that'd been his gift all of these years. He remembered the way that they'd met 35 years ago. It had been at a funeral, her father was a pastor and Bertus' mother had passed on. Bertus had never stepped foot in a church before, except on the day of his mother's funeral. His mother had committed suicide, after 27 years of being with a du Toit, she'd done as many other women in the family had done, taken a gun to her head and blew her brains out. It's said that's the only way they could escape the du Toit men. Rosita was the pastor's daughter. She was a quiet and devoted good girl, and he knew from the moment that their eyes met as he was walking up to his mother's closed casket that she was his and he stopped at nothing to have her.

He looked at her now, in the 35 years that they'd been together, she'd changed. She was no longer the girl that he'd met, but it was impossible for any woman to stay the same after being claimed by a du Toit. She'd changed, become a different woman that he still loved and cared for. Over the years the once innocent face of the 19 year old girl he'd met at the Evangelist Church in Valhalla had matured into the now 54 year old woman who'd given him two perfect sons and a woman who'd always stood by his side. The innocent gleam in her eyes was no more, the softness of her features changed over time, after all of the lessons she'd learned, those eyes never shed tears anymore.

"My love," he began, removing the glasses off his face to look at the angry woman before him.

"N-no!" she snapped, "No, you don't get to call me that," she continued angrily, her voice carrying with a coldness that could cause a reverse effect on the climate. "Who is she, Bertus?" she repeated the question.

Johannes who was seated beside his father, watched on through his peripheral vision, glancing at his father and mother as he heard the sounds of his brother's wife's screams as she gave birth. Johannes smoothed his hand over the front of his suit, bringing the other with the bitter tea to his lips and drinking from it.

Bertus didn't respond to the question, he just looked at his wife. He's so much like his son, so much like Schalk, Rosita thought, as she felt every bit of her resolve crumble into nothing but boiling anger. "He did this to me! Your own son, he taught me a lesson," she brought her hand up, showing him her hand and showing him the tongue that had been sliced off, probably swimming in the sewers somewhere after she'd taken a shit.

Bertus knew about Schalk teaching Rosita a lesson, "you should've known better than to touch what was his," Bertus explained to his wife, coldly, putting his reading glasses back on his eyes and paying attention to the contract that his son, Johannes had brought for him to read over.

Rosita grabbed the contract from between his hands and threw it across the room, the papers flying every which way, "Bertus, I know you," she said, looking at him with fiery eyes, "I know you, Bertus. You would've never allowed for Schalk, or anyone to put their hands on me, ever," She stressed the heavy words that she'd been wanting to say to him for a week now, "it wouldn't matter what I did, Bertus. I've done worse, but this, this lets me know that there's someone else, so who the fuck is she?" her voice raised with each word as Bertus fell silent and removed his glasses from his face.

He looked to where his wife had thrown the papers and opted to bring the cup of coffee mixed with whisky to his lips, drinking from it. "Where have you been, Bertus? You're not coming home anymore, and don't you dare fucking say it's work when you've been working for 35 years of our marriage and have always come home to me! You always come home to me! And you always take me with you on your business trips, so who the fuck is she?!" Rosita wasn't a silly woman, she knew Bertus du Toit like the back of her hand, they'd been together for 35 years and she'd always known that she was his gift.

Being his gift meant that he wanted her by his side always, and that no harm would ever come to her. She'd gotten used to it but now, things felt different between the two of them.

For a few days now, he'd been disinterested in her, his eyes no longer holding the dark glare in them when he looked at her. There was usually a look of possession in his eyes that had become like love to her and it'd become home to her. She loved it because she knew that she meant everything to him. He'd bring the world to his knees for her and hurt her if she dared to get away from him. His love had become like a drug to her and now, he was withdrawing.

To outsiders, they wouldn't understand. Being his gift, being a du Toit's gift became like oxygen to her and without it, she wouldn't live. To others they'd think that her husband was simply cheating on her, but a du Toit never cheated, nothing was more important than their gift. To a du Toit, once you were their gift, there was no going back. The only thing that could capture the attention of a du Toit, was a gift; another woman. She knew that there was someone else, another gift. Had he tired of her? Was she so old that he needed another? Or had she never been a gift? Had he found another gift?

She screamed, seeing him being as nonchalant as she saw him now– seeing in his eyes the absence of his obsession, seeing in his actions how uncaring he was that she was hurt. She grabbed her bag and began beating him with it, swinging it side to side as she screeched at the top of her lungs, feeling every bit of emotion she'd never felt before come to the surface; anger, jealousy, heartbreak, fear, disgust; there weren't enough words to describe them, so she kept swinging the bag, meeting his face each time, attacking him as much as she could.

"That's not fair!" she yelled with each hit, "it's not fair! It's not fair!" tears fell from her eyes, pain dripping from her words as he gripped the bag and snatched it out of her hold and she resorted to hitting him with her hands. She knew that she couldn't hurt him but she prayed that she could, hoped that she could hurt him like he'd hurt her, like he was hurting her.

"You," she sobbed, slapping him, "fucking," her hands were everywhere as she cried, "bastard!" wails wrecked her body as she stumbled back from him, wanting to look into his eyes, wanting to see if he felt a bit of pain at watching her crumble like she was at the moment, but he was unmoved. Bertus remained silent, his blue eyes on the coffee that had spilled everywhere. He tossed the empty cup to the floor and then looked at his wife who looked like she knew of his secret.

He cleared his throat, "I'm sorry," he found himself finally letting out– watching the way that tears flowed down her face. He'd thought that she was his gift and he'd done all that he could to keep her to him. The burning fire he'd felt for her, felt like only a spark when it came to the woman that he'd recently crossed paths with. In all the years that he'd been with his wife, he'd had no desire to be with any other woman, to cheat on her, to leave her, or to love Rosita any less. The woman that he'd met now, she brought something else out of him, a darkness unlike any other– a darkness he'd never experienced before. It was eating him alive, gnawing at him, peeling through his skin and bursting out of him, the flames of the desire that he felt for her, the flames of the darkness burned him to ashes. He knew then, that the woman, Precious, was his true gift.

Bertus guessed he did owe Rosita an apology, after so many years of believing that she was his gift and giving so much of her life to him, it'd all been a mistake.

"No! No!" her screams echoed throughout the hospital, rivalling those of Zama Ivy as Rosita felt her knees almost give from under her as she felt the room begin to spin around her and the walls begin to close in around her. She could hear the screams of her father, the screams of her mother as Bertus tortured them to teach her a lesson, and she could hear her own screams of terror as he tortured her, teaching her lessons because she dared to run away from him. "You don't get to ruin me!" her voice was raw and hurt, her wails one of a woman who was getting her heart broken all over again, "You don't get to ruin me and say you're sorry! You fucking ruined me, Bertus! You said that I was your gift! My father, my mother, my sister," she listed, "they all died because of you! You killed them! Killed them because you said that I was your gift!"

Rosita was reliving every horrible moment that she'd pretended never existed so that she could face the man before her. The sound of cries, the sound of wails, the sound of pleas, the sound of skin burning, the sound of her parents drawing their last breath, the sound of Bertus telling her that she was his; everything– she was reliving it all.

She had her hands to her ears, blocking them as if to block out all of that noise that now flooded her brain. She lost her grip on reality and flung herself at Bertus, realising all that he'd taken from her only for him to be wrong, only for him to be sorry. "Bring it back! Bring them all back! Bring me back! You're a fucking monster!" she clawed at him, gripped a handful of his hair in between her teeth, attempting to attack him as much as she could, she kicked her heels into his stomach and screeched like a banshee. "No! No! Let me go!" Security and some doctors had rushed into the area to restrain the maddened woman and pull Rosita off Bertus.

She continued to scream and cry, "It's not fair! It's not fair! No! How could you, Bertus?! I gave you life! I gave you every-thing, even if you took everything from me! I've got scars! Scars because of you!" she wailed, her heart broken words meeting the ears of all those around her, "I'll fucking kill you, Bertus! I'll fucking kill you! I swear, I'm going to kill you! All of you! Let me go! Let me kill him!" A female doctor rushed forward with a syringe, driving it deep in her neck, making Rosita fight less and less, "no...n-no...ple-please...you, you don-don't understand..." she weakly argued as the drugs began to kick in, "it's the curse...the curse..."

In the room where the door had been closed, right down the hall, came the cries of a new born baby, and happy smiles, "it's twins!" the doctor said with a grin as he handed the baby to Schalk whose hand felt like it was going to fall off at any moment due to how hard Ivy had been squeezing it as she was giving birth, "a boy, and a girl!"

Schalk felt his heart soar with a level of happiness and love that overcame his entire being as he looked down at the tiny bundle in his arms. His little girl was bloody and dirty, but even in that state, she was perfect. He peered down at her and then rushed over to his wife where the doctor's had placed his son on Ivy's naked chest.

Ivy looked at the perfect, tiny human being on her chest before she peered up at her husband, the two of them making eye contact and sharing something greater than words at the moment. "She's perfect," Ivy croaked out, her eyes on her baby girl, her mind completely forgotten about the pain that she'd just gone through as her heart swelled with a level of love that she knew tied her to the little girl forever.

Schalk leaned down and pressed a kiss to her lips, "she's our little Daisy-Bloom."

Schalk then looked at his son, his first born son. "She'd been eating up most of the food in the womb and that should explain why he looks frail, and why we didn't pick up the baby during screening. It's a miracle, really," Dr Ahmed said with a smile, explaining to the new-parents who now had two babies.

"I have a son..." Schalk spoke, his eyes on the perfect human being in his wife's arms. Every du Toit men pictured the day that they would bring a son into this world, a true du Toit, to live on the name and to strengthen it. Schalk's sweet Ivy had given him the greatest gift of all, she was a gift that kept on giving; an heir. A son that he would raise, a son that he would teach the ways of being a du Toit. He hadn't been eating in the womb as the doctors were explaining, and he looked frail and thin, but pride burst in Schalk's chest; survivor. His son was a survivor, the best trait of a du Toit. "Du Toit," Schalk finally spoke, retreating from his mind and looking down at the first of the next generation of his lineage, "Mathys du Toit."